D*U*C*K

D*U*C*K

A tale of men, birds, and one's purpose in life

Poppy Z. Brite

Subterranean Press ★ 2006

First Edition

ISBN-10: 1-59606-076-x
ISBN-13: 978-1-59606-076-0

Subterranean Press
PO Box 190106
Burton, MI 48519

www.subterraneanpress.com

This story is dedicated to the memory
of Buddy Diliberto,
alive in New Orleans hearts forever;
and to Bobby Hebert,
the only act who could follow him.

WHERE THE STORM NEVER HAPPENED (FOR NOW)

A few words about D*U*C*K

Anew body of literature has begun to emerge from New Orleans, South Louisiana, and the Gulf Coast. It's known as "Katriniana," and I've collected almost every piece of it published so far. This book, however, is not part of it.

After the storm and catastrophic flooding of 2005, I initially thought I would never want to write about these events. I wanted to keep writing about the New Orleans I had loved, a city that had never been destroyed. I wanted my Liquorverse to continue as I had known it, even if nothing else in my life could. I soon came to see that this would be not only irresponsible and callous, but impossible. For those of us who lived and continue to live in New Orleans, these events are all we've thought about for months. They will continue to haunt us and change our lives forever. Of course I would have to write about them.

But not just yet.

D*U*C*K is the first piece of original fiction I've completed since the storm. I think of it as slightly-alternate-universe fiction, a kind of fairy tale set in the same world of chefs and restaurants I've been writing about for several years now, but in which the storm didn't come to New Orleans. Maybe it took a different path (there's a slight hint of this in the story), maybe it never entered the Gulf in the first place. I plan to deal with it in the next Liquor novel, *Dead Shrimp Blues,* and probably another one after that. Just for now, though, I wanted to write a story where the one-eyed bitch wasn't a factor. Doing so was a balm for my soul and helped me get closer to the time when I will have to read all that Katriniana I've collected and write some of my own.

I've taken a couple of minor fictional liberties with the lovely little town of Opelousas, but Ducks Unlimited (www.ducks.org) is a real organization, an excellent one that promotes the conservation of coastal wetlands and other waterbird habitat. Protection of these wetlands probably could have prevented much of the devastation from Hurricanes Katrina and Rita and, if carried out in a more responsible fashion than in the past, could help prevent future tragedy. Dave Hammond, the badly behaved waiter at the beginning of this tale, is named for a reader who won an eBay auction to have a character named after him. 100% of the proceeds from the auction went to Ducks Unlimited. Thanks to Dave, and also to Henry Barber, The Boudin Link (www.boudinlink.com), Gene Broussard, Cathy Campanella, Chris DeBarr, Joel L. Fletcher, Kris LaMorte, Kevin Maroney, the Palace Café of Opelousas, Greg Peters, Bill Schafer, and Carl Walker. For information on the New Orleans Lakefront Airport, I am indebted to Mark Grady for his May 5, 2005 article in *The Southern Aviator.*

—Poppy Z. Brite,
New Orleans, May 2006

RICKEY TAKES OUT THE TRASH

Everything you've heard about summer in New Orleans is true. The only tourists who visit during that infernal season are hardy Germans and Australians, who can weather anything, and people from Alabama, Mississippi, and Texas, who are used to it and don't have far to drive. The deepest pits of Hades have nothing on your average August day in the Crescent City. (You can say Crescent City if you like, because the Mississippi River cups the city in a crescent shape. Say "the Big Easy," or, worse, "N'Awlins," and people will know you're a tourist.)

Because of the sun pounding down out of the coppery sky—because of the stickiness that turns the air into a dish-cloth from which you feel certain you could wring dirty water if only you could catch hold of it—because of that stink that rises off sidewalks and asphalt parking lots, choking the unwary with ghosts of shrimp shells, dogshit, burning tires and armpits—because the temperature seldom drops below the high eighties even at midnight, the people of the city try to keep their physical exertions to a minimum. In the heat of the day, there might be one old white man in a seersucker suit moving snail-slow along a sidewalk, or a group of black teenagers gesturing languidly at each other on the corner. Certainly there will be an ancient woman carrying a shopping bag and an umbrella; there's no chance of rain, but she's using the thing for a sunshade. These folks, you expect to see. The middle-aged man in the Broad Street neutral ground, standing motionless with a sign in each hand, occasionally putting one of them down to take out a handkerchief and blot the sweat from his smooth ebony dome—he is an unusual sight. His signs are handmade, but neatly printed. One reads **THOU SHALT NOT KILL**. The other says **ENOUGH IS ENOUGH**. You don't see him every day, but if you're from New Orleans or know the city well, you understand immediately what he's talking about.

There will be these people, and somewhere nearby there will be a chef hard at work. Kitchen workers don't have the option of keeping their labors to a minimum. Through sweat-soaked Julys and Augusts they preside over stovetop flames and the hot breath of ovens, swampy dish sinks and desert heat-mirages rising off grills.

On this particular August day, a hard-headed chef named John Rickey was taking out a bag of wet trash, muttering and cursing over it with no idea that a few minutes from now he would be wishing his head were a little harder. He was muttering and cursing not because he thought a chef-owner was too good to take out the trash—he knew better than that—but because he had told one of the low cooks on his kitchen totem pole to do it an hour ago, and the cook hadn't done it. Devonte was a hell of a lot more seasoned than he had been when Rickey hired him, but occasionally he just sort of...spaced. It might mean he was thinking about the tricked-out car he hoped to buy, or the pussy he hoped to score at his favorite hip-hop club, or nothing at all. This time of year, it might also mean he was looking forward to the beginning of the basketball season, in which case Rickey's partner and co-chef, G-man, would probably be looking forward to it right along with him. But G-man wouldn't space; G-man was the solidest cook in the kitchen.

The whole crew was solid, even Devonte and the new kid, Jacolvy, most of the time. Still, Rickey missed Devonte's predecessor, Shake, with whom he and G-man had been working for years. Shake had snagged a sweet sous chef position at La Pharmacie, a hot new restaurant on Magazine Street. The chef over there had basically poached him from Rickey's restaurant, Liquor, but Rickey didn't hold it against Shake: there wasn't much room for advancement at Liquor and Shake had given them a good three years. He wished he had Shake back just for tonight, though; there were three major conventions in town, Liquor had two-fifty on the books, and they were going to get hammered.

Half-absorbed in these thoughts, still muttering about the trash, Rickey heaved the bag up and over the edge of the Dumpster. The ripe sour-milk smell of garbage wafted toward him, but he barely noticed it; just as the zookeeper ceases to smell elephant shit, this was one of the normal odors of his life. He was turning to go back into the restaurant when his world exploded with a tremendous crack that seemed to come from inside his skull. He felt his knees connect with the concrete apron around the Dumpsters. His field of vision went red, then turned to a field of glittering silver and blue stars that seemed to drip through the air before his eyes like fireworks… except that his eyes were closed, weren't they? While he was thinking about this, the pain arrived, a huge pair of pincers that grabbed him by the temples and squeezed. Faintly he could hear somebody yelling: "How you like it now, you fucking faggot? You shitfuck! How you like it now, asshole?" Rickey tried to lift his hand to the back of his head where the pain seemed most concentrated—if his fingers encountered wetness and a hole, he would know he'd been shot—but before he could get his arm up, another explosion came. This one bounced his forehead off the concrete, and he passed out.

THE LURKER BY THE DUMPSTERS

Rickey's croutons were burning. G-man could smell them from all the way across the kitchen, where he was prepping fresh porcini mushrooms to go with tonight's duck special. "Rickey!" he hollered. "You got shit on fire in here!"

No answer. G-man sighed, crossed the kitchen, and pulled the sheet pan of croutons out of the oven. They were a few shades darker than they probably should have been, but with everything else that needed to be done today, he wasn't going to throw them out. Where was Rickey, though? It wasn't like him to walk off and leave his prep work to die.

"Rickey!" he yelled again.

"I think he took out the trash," said Devonte, coming in from the hall that led to the walk-in cooler, employee restroom, and office.

"Coulda sworn I heard him tell *you* to take out the trash a while ago."

Devonte looked away. "I got to doin somethin else and forgot. Sorry."

"Yeah, well, I just want to know where Rickey is."

G-man laid his knife on the cutting board and headed for the back door, limping a little on the foot that had been bothering him for a couple of months now. It was no big deal, just a bone that felt like it was going to pop out of place every now and then. If he sat down for a minute and flexed his toes the right way, it usually faded to a dull ache. He had just turned thirty-two, Rickey would catch up with him in September, and they had been working in kitchens since they were fifteen: plenty of time to build up a generous assortment of aches, pains, scars, and calluses.

He whacked the pressure bar and stuck his head out the back door, expecting to see Rickey talking to some purveyor who'd just pulled up with an order: that seemed the likeliest thing to delay him. Instead, G-man couldn't immediately process what he was seeing. Because his eyes were weak and light-sensitive, he always wore dark glasses in the kitchen, and for the first couple of seconds after he opened the door, the relentless sunlight blinded him: he just saw dark shapes and bright patches. Then the picture resolved into something horrible. Rickey was lying prone on the ground between the Dumpsters and the restaurant, his face against the hot asphalt. A big guy was standing over him kicking him in the ribs. Lying on the ground beside Rickey's head was a two-by-four with a smear of blood on it.

G-man turned in the half-open doorway as if he was planning to go back into the restaurant. "TERRANCE!" he shouted as loud as he could. "HELP ME!" Then he darted back around the door and into the parking lot. The guy had already taken off running, but G-man caught him easily, rabbit-punched him in the back of the neck, then spun him around and kneed him in the balls. The guy staggered for a second, then fell to the asphalt groaning.

G-man ran back to Rickey. Terrance, their 280-pound grill guy, was already there. "Grab that asshole!" G-man panted.

"Don't let him get away!" He dropped to one knee beside Rickey, who was already trying to push himself up onto his forearms. A thin trickle of blood ran from one nostril and his eyes were like twin zeroes in a slot-machine window. "Fucker got the drop on me," he mumbled. "Burned my fucking croutons."

"Yeah, you did. Don't worry about it. Here, lay your head on my leg."

Rickey did, and blood began to soak into the houndstooth fabric of G-man's chef pants. Meanwhile, Terrance had lifted Mr. Two-By-Four as easily as he would a fifty-pound sack of oysters and dragged him back over to the Dumpsters. "You know this asshole?" he said, cuffing the guy on the side of the head to make him turn his face toward G-man.

G-man found it hard to look away from Rickey, but he made himself squint up at the guy's face. Yes, he realized; he *did* know this asshole. Had, in fact, handed him his last paycheck not two weeks ago, after Rickey had fired him.

Rickey wasn't too tyrannical as far as bosses went, but he had a few strict rules, most of which were directed at waiters and other front-of-the-house staff. It wasn't that he failed to discipline his kitchen crew, but that he tended to hire kitchen people he already knew he could trust. The front of the house was trickier. Neither Rickey nor G-man had much experience handling it; as lifelong kitchen guys, they were naturally suspicious of waiters, whom they secretly believed to work half as hard as cooks and make twice as much money. The waiters sensed this ill-concealed animosity, and the turnover rate among Liquor's servers was higher than Rickey and G-man would like it to be.

One of Rickey's most holy rules had to do with chewing gum in the dining room. Some of the servers liked to do it so they wouldn't breathe halitosis fumes on the customers, but Rickey thought it looked tacky and forbade it. He even bought tins of Altoids and left them at the wait station, which mostly got the message across, but apparently this guy—Dave, G-man remembered, his name was Dave Hammond—didn't care for Altoids. The first time Rickey saw him chewing gum on the floor, he gave him a warning. The second time, he lurked in wait behind the kitchen door, and when Dave came through, Rickey smacked him on the back of the head so hard that the wad of gum flew out of his mouth and stuck to the opposite wall. Only Dave's pride had been hurt, but apparently the message still hadn't gotten through, because Rickey caught him folding a stick of gum into his mouth during service a couple of weeks later and gave him his walking papers.

Rickey and G-man had grown up in the Lower Ninth Ward, one of the scrappier parts of a generally scrappy city, and knew how to hold their own in a street fight. G-man was a basically peaceful soul, but even after having most of his rough edges smoothed off by the comparatively genteel world of restaurant ownership, Rickey was maybe a little too inclined to use his fists. No waiter could have put him on the ground in a fair fight, G-man knew that much. Guy must have hidden behind the Dumpsters and waited for Rickey.

"Call the cops," he said to Devonte, who'd just come out the back door. Then he glanced down at Rickey, who was bleeding freely from a gash on the back of his head. "And an ambulance."

"No cops," Rickey gasped. "No ambulance." By gripping G-man's forearm, he managed to lever himself into a kneeling position. Those twin-zero eyes settled on the bloody two-by-four. He groped for it, grabbed one end, and, using it like a cane, pushed himself to his feet. G-man hovered behind him, ready to catch him if he went over backwards. Instead he advanced on Dave and half-raised the board. The waiter struggled in Terrance's massive grip.

"How many times he hit you?" said Terrance. "I'll let you get your fair licks, but I ain't gonna hold him while you beat his head in."

"Let me go, you damn…"

Terrance put his face close to Dave's. "Damn *what?*"

The waiter seemed to consider what he could get away with. "Dishwasher," he said finally.

Terrance laughed. "Ain't been a dishwasher for three years now. Not since that guy you just clobbered hired me to work the grill."

Rickey took another step, hesitated, then dropped the board, spun, and stumbled. G-man caught him by the waist-band of his pants and held him as he doubled over and threw up on the side of one of the Dumpsters.

Approaching sirens split the heat of the day. Terrance met G-man's eyes and sighed. "Ain't this some kinda fuckarow," he said.

III

RICKEY CALLS THE WRONG PLAY

These sounds, even in the haze:

The familiar engine of G-man's old Mercury, chugging steadily. Apparently he or somebody else had convinced G-man to dispense with the ambulance.

(what ambulance?)

The streetcar, rattling along its track; from its proximity, he could tell it was the St. Charles line, not the new one on Canal.

A hollow ringing in his head that seemed to emanate from the very spot where the board had hit him.

(what board?!)

G-man's voice, cutting through the fog. "Dude, we're here. C'mon, can you stand up? Just hang onto my arm. Jeez, he really got you good. I can't wait to put his ass in jail."

"G...I was just taking out the trash...I must've fell and hit my head..."

"*Somebody* hit your head, awright. C'mon, look, be careful on these stairs." G-man's strong arm encircled his waist and practically boosted him up a small flight of stairs.

"Where are we? We gotta get back to the restaurant, dude, we got two-fifty on the books."

"I know it," G-man said grimly, but he kept hustling Rickey along, through a door and up another flight of stairs. At the top of that flight was a big, airy room where Rickey was allowed to sit down again. He grayed back out for a while.

The next thing he knew, a searchlight was probing his left eye. "He's pretty groggy," said the voice of God. Rickey didn't believe in God, but he knew G-man did. Were they in church? They'd better not be, if G-man knew what was good for him. It didn't make sense anyway; why would G-man make him go to church when his head was hurting so bad?

"Yeah," said G-man. "What about all that blood?"

"Oh, that's nothing. Scalp wounds bleed like a bastard."

Would God say "bleed like a bastard," if he were real? Rickey didn't think so, but he wasn't sure.

"I'll get the nurse to clean it up and put some Dermabond on it. Nothing to worry about."

"Who are you?" he managed.

A face resolved itself in his vision, old and bearded but not enough of either to be God. "Dr. Herbst. Your friend Lenny Duveteaux called me, asked me to squeeze you in so you wouldn't have to go to the emergency room. I owe Lenny a couple favors."

"Everybody owes Lenny a couple favors."

"See," the doctor told G-man, "he's starting to make sense."

The doctor had that Uptown New Orleans drawl that tried to sound Southern and didn't quite make it. He'd never say "awright" for "all right" or "axe" for "ask"; that was for lower-class downtowners like Rickey and G-man. They'd moved up to Marengo Street years ago, well within the boundaries of Uptown, but their Brooklynese speech would forever mark them as Lower Ninth Warders.

"Any blurred vision?" The doctor held up a newspaper in front of Rickey's face. "What's the headline say?"

"'ANOTHER NEAR MISS.'" A category-5 hurricane in the Gulf had jagged northeast and gone to Florida last week.

"What's the caption?"

"Some shit about morons buying bottled water and plywood."

"I really think he's OK," the doctor told G-man. "Cracked his coconut pretty good, but as long as he rests in bed for a couple days, he'll be fine."

Rickey's eyes met G-man's. G-man was still wearing his customary shades, but Rickey could see the alarm behind them.

"Can't rest," Rickey said. "We got two-fifty on the books."

"Excuse me?"

"Reservations," G-man explained. "Two hundred fifty customers." He took a deep breath, then said bravely, "But it doesn't matter, Rickey. You gotta go home and rest."

"Yeah, right, and you gotta bite my crank. I'm working tonight. If I keel over, you can drag me off the line and dump me in the walk-in to cool down. I'm not laying on my ass at home while y'all get slammed."

He stared at Herbst, expecting an argument, but the doctor just shrugged. "It's your head. You've got a concussion, but if you think you can work, you probably can. Might want to keep a bucket nearby—you'll likely make yourself sick."

"A concussion!" said G-man.

"It's no big deal," Rickey said. "Remember that Saints game in '89, when they played Tampa Bay? Bobby Hebert got a real bad concussion, but then the backup quarterback got hurt too and Bobby went back in. Played the rest of the game. He was a fucking iron man."

"Did they win?"

"Well, no. And he called a couple wrong plays, plays he had in college. But he didn't, like, die or anything."

G-man frowned but offered no further argument. *If you can stand, you can work* was part of the cooks' gospel.

The cops had wanted Rickey to come to the police station and make a statement about the attack, but he managed to convince them he didn't want to press charges. As far as he was concerned, the beef was between him and Dave Hammond: he'd smacked the waiter on the back of the head, the waiter had smacked him back a little harder. If he ever saw Dave again, Rickey would probably take him down, but whining to cops and judges was for sissies. Even so, dinner service had already begun by the time they got back to Liquor. G-man came around to help Rickey out of the car, and Rickey gripped G-man's shoulder, steadying himself.

"You sure you gonna be OK?"

"I better be, huh?" Rickey touched the swollen lump on the back of his head and grimaced. "I'm just embarrassed that a fucking *waiter* got the drop on me, that's all. It was a fair fight, I'd a kicked his ass into the middle of next week."

"Course you would. Like you even need to tell me that."

They entered the restaurant through the back door and walked into the kitchen. The crew was already busy with the first wave of early diners, but as soon as they saw Rickey, they all stopped whatever they were doing, put down their knives and spatulas, and broke into applause.

"Aw, now, what the fuck?" said Rickey, but he was grinning.

"Thickest skull in New Orleans!" Terrance hollered.

"You wanna get the drop on Rickey, you gotta sneak up behind him and hit him with a damn *plank!*" This from Tanker, their pastry guy.

"Plank, hell," said Devonte. "That was the whole *tree!*"

"And Rickey was still ready to kick his ass!" That was Marquis, who'd been the freshest meat in the kitchen before they hired Devonte and loved to lord it over the poor kid.

"OK, OK." Rickey held up his hands. "Yeah, I'm ready to work, but I feel kinda wobbly on my feet. Y'all gotta help me out tonight, keep an eye on what I do, let me know if I fuck something up. OK?"

"We're always ready to let you know if you fuck something up," said Tanker. "Not that you ever admit it when you do."

Rickey took his customary place at the expediting station. The expediter stood at the front of the kitchen, called out orders to the various stations as the tickets came out of the printer, and put the finishing touches on plates just before they went out to the dining room. In automotive terms, he was both the kitchen's driver and its steering column. G-man, at the sauté station, was the carburetor; taking raw materials and turning them into finished dishes, he produced the majority of the food that came out of this kitchen. Marquis wasn't yet seasoned enough to work sauté by himself, but he was assisting G-man tonight, a sort of booster fuel. Terrance at the grill, Tanker in his dessert nook, and Devonte at the cold-appetizer station were wheels; while their role wasn't as close to the heart of kitchen as G-man's, the car wouldn't go anywhere without them. And the diners were the network of streets upon which the car traveled; they weren't central to the design of the vehicle, but without them, it would have nowhere to go.

(The front of the house, as far as Rickey was concerned, was the old coot who drove twenty miles an hour right in front of you on a road with no passing lane. Today's events had not improved his view of this unavoidable but highly irksome facet of restaurant life.)

The night went smoothly enough at first. Dr. Herbst had given Rickey a vitamin shot, which didn't have much to do with his head but had pepped him up a little. As it wore off, the tickets seemed to proliferate and blur before his eyes. He could still read them, but he had to squint to keep the letters from jiggling wildly all over the little slips of paper. He had to stop and think about how to finish each plate, normally an automatic process: did the chervil sprigs go on the redfish or the softshell crab? Was it the pork or the mackerel that got a dash of chili oil from the squeeze bottle? Several dishes needed more than one final touch, and that increased his confusion. The kitchen was very hot, very bright, very loud. He began to feel nauseous, but stepped on that in a hurry: he could get sick later. Instead he pulled another ticket from the printer and scowled at it. The words sizzled and danced, but he thought he could make them out. "G," he called, "ordering one Indian lamb shank, two lobster with fried spinach, one stuffed quail."

The kitchen sucked in its collective breath. The cooks were too busy to really stop what they were doing, but there was a slight, hushed pause that would have been undetectable to anyone not familiar with their rhythms.

"Dude," G-man said at last, "those aren't dishes we have. Those are *Peychaud Grill* dishes."

The Peychaud Grill was where Rickey and G-man had earned their chops. They'd worked in a bunch of restaurants before that, but the Peychaud Grill and its chef, Paco Valdeon, turned them from half-assed hot-line meat into formidable cooks. The Peychaud had gone down in flames and been closed for years now, with Paco variously reported to be cooking on the beach in Mexico, running cocaine in South America, or dead. Whatever had become of him, he would always be Rickey's first real chef, the one who had not just given him permission to be serious about food but shown him that there was no acceptable alternative.

Evidently Paco's dishes were hardwired into some reptilian part of Rickey's brain, accessible even when his own creations had begun to fail him. He wondered if he might actually have some kind of brain damage, but tried to brush the thought aside; there was no time to worry about that right now and anyway he had never been MENSA material. Instead he made a monumental effort to collect himself, and then G-man was there beside him, gripping the meaty part of his arm: "Dude, what do you need? I think I better stay on sauté, you don't have the energy for that, but I could put Devonte on desserts and let you take his station, and Tanker could expedite, or—"

"No. I'm fine. I can do it."

"You're *not* fine. Look, I'm not mad, I'm just worried, but you're calling out orders from ten years ago. That's not fine and you know it."

"Yeah, I know it. But let me just get my shit together, G. Anything else happens, I'll go be a pantry bitch."

"You sure?"

"Yeah."

"OK." G-man's eyes were doubtful, but Rickey knew he couldn't afford to hang around discussing it. "I better go get my own shit together, then, before everything crashes and burns."

Rickey wanted nothing more than to hook an arm around G-man's neck and let G-man lead him out of the overbright, pulsing hell his own kitchen had become, but instead he just said, "Sure. Go on."

As G-man walked back to the sauté station—limping slightly, Rickey noticed; damn, but they were a gimpy crew tonight—a young waiter named Tommy peered through the pass. "Hey, Chef?"

"Yeah?" Rickey scowled at him, expecting an earful of woe about how long his tables had been waiting for their entrées or the like.

Instead, Tommy stuck his arm through the pass. Cupped in the palm of his hand was a tiny pocket mirror, and on the mirror's surface were a cut-down drinking straw and a short line of cocaine. "I know you're having a rough night because of what Dave did," the waiter said. "I just wanted you to know that some of us are on your side."

Rickey gave him a long look, then bent over, picked up the straw, and snorted the coke without taking the mirror from Tommy's hand. "Thanks," he said. "How they looking out there?"

"Oh, drunk. They'll be all right."

Rickey's vision seemed to miraculously clear as he looked at the row of fresh tickets. He hadn't had cocaine in years, wasn't a big fan of the stuff, but right now it was hitting the spot. *Just what the doctor ordered,* Rickey thought, and laughed aloud to think of the useless Dr. Herbst prescribing it. *Take one bump and call me in the morning.* Maybe he could get through this night after all.

GALL AND WORMWOOD

G-man saw Tommy at the pass with something shiny in his hand, saw Rickey bend over the waiter's outstretched arm, shiver a little, then straighten his shoulders and scan the tickets in front of him with renewed confidence. He guessed what Rickey was doing and rolled his eyes, but he couldn't get too worked up about it. After all, Paco Valdeon had been quite the coke fiend. Maybe Rickey needed to get into Paco mode to survive this shift.

"Yo, G," said Terrance from his spot behind the grill.

"Yo, T."

"What you call this veal bone sauce again?"

"Um, avocadomeno."

"AVGOLEMONO," Rickey shouted. "Jesus Christ! It doesn't have anything to do with avocadoes. It's a classic Greek egg-lemon sauce, except ours has Citron vodka. Morons."

It's the coke talking, G-man silently reminded himself. He looked forward to the time when the coke would shut up, but as long as Rickey could expedite in a way that made some kind of sense, he didn't particularly care if Rickey acted like an asshole. He hoped the drug wouldn't interact badly with the knock on the head Rickey had taken, but as long as Rickey didn't keel over dead, things could hardly get worse than having your expediter call out dishes that weren't on the menu.

"And we serving it with ouzo, right?" said Terrance, tipping G-man a wink.

"ORZO!" Rickey bellowed, unable to see that Terrance was messing with him. "Orzo pasta. Jesus fucking *Christ!*"

It was a long slog of a night. In the end, G-man could find nothing in it to be proud of except that nobody had walked out and only two diners had sent their food back. One of those was a steak Rickey had called out mid-rare when the diner had ordered it mid-well, and people who ordered their steaks mid-well often took a perverse delight in sending them back to be further incinerated, so that wasn't too terrible. The other was worse: an entrée Rickey had simply forgotten to order, one of a six-top. The other five diners had gotten their food while the poor woman sat and stewed. The kitchen made her duck special on the fly, but by the time the waiter got it to the table, she was drunk and belligerent and simply refused to eat it. "I guess she showed *us!*" the waiter had cackled, cramming the succulent slices of duck breast into his mouth, but G-man felt bad about it: that woman would have unpleasant memories of Liquor forever, would tell anyone who'd listen about her deplorable evening there. The flawless appetizer she'd eaten would become gall and wormwood in her memory. The free drinks the waiter had plied her with would only haze her anguish a little.

The coke had long since worn off by the time they broke down the kitchen, and G-man was able to get Rickey home without much trouble. They sat slumped at their kitchen table, Rickey gingerly feeling the goose egg on the back of his skull, G-man just staring at the white ceramic tabletop because anything more stimulating would overtax his mind. "You sure you're OK?" he asked Rickey finally.

"Yeah, man, I'm fine."

G-man made a fist. "How many fingers I'm holding up?"

Rickey laughed, reached across the table for G-man's hand, brought it to his lips, and kissed one of the many fine white scars on the knuckles. "For real, I'm fine," he said. "I got a head too hard for any goddamn waiter to crack."

"I guess you do."

The sheets on their bed sometimes got a funky smell from too many nights of coming home and falling into them without showering off the kitchen grime, but Rickey had changed them the day before and they were still crisp and clean. G-man expected to be asleep as soon as his head hit the pillow, but instead he lay awake for a long time, listening to Rickey's even breathing and wondering what he would have done if the guy had seriously hurt Rickey. All at once he was engulfed in a white-hot, pounding rage almost completely foreign to him. He felt as if he'd just taken a punch to the chest, had to work to catch his breath. Jesus. Rickey talked about being pissed off all the time. Was this how he felt? G-man didn't see how anybody could stand it.

He closed his eyes, folded his hands across his chest, and muttered under his breath, "OurFatherwhoartinheavenhallowedbethynamethykingdomcomethywillbedone—" After years of being estranged from the Church of his childhood, he had started to come back to it a little. Not the endless dogma and rigmarole, but the deep quiet place he was able find inside himself on the rare occasions when he went to Mass. He wasn't entirely comfortable with this renewed faith, attraction, reprogramming, or whatever it was, and Rickey, who took certain of the Church's positions as personal affronts, loathed it. Still, after all that had happened today, he couldn't help but offer up his thanks for Rickey's extraordinarily thick skull.

Without warning or logic, G-man found himself thinking of their first kiss. They'd been sixteen, in Rickey's bedroom,

Rickey's mother away for the weekend. G-man had simultaneously known and not known it was going to happen; it seemed both inconceivable and inevitable. When Rickey finally did lean over and kiss him, G-man's hand had risen as if of its own accord to cup the back of Rickey's head, not wanting him to draw away. He realized as his fingers twined in it that he had never touched Rickey's hair before. It was silky but slightly tangled, as Rickey and his hairbrush had only the most passing of acquaintances. That hadn't changed in all these years.

The details, the memories, the automatic gestures and associations incomprehensible to anyone outside the hermetic twosome of the relationship—these were the things G-man could not imagine losing when something, against his will, made him contemplate losing Rickey. No one else in the world would remember that kiss, how scary it had been and yet how the world had opened wide around them, infinite with possibilities that hadn't existed the instant before. Where would all that go if one of *them* were gone?

No. Better to hope, at least, that there could be some kind of permanence, some link that survived. And that, G-man's sister Rosalie had once told him, was one of the reasons why you kept saying the prayers even when you weren't sure you believed in them.

He said another Our Father, more slowly this time, really thinking about the words. He could forgive those who trespassed against him; he'd never been able to hold much of a grudge. But those who trespassed against Rickey? That was harder, that was the test.

Suddenly he wanted to wake Rickey up, wanted Rickey wrapped around him, on top of him, inside him as intensely as he ever had. His gut clenched with an atavistic, purely sexual desire; his heart cried for Rickey, craving the physical and emotional engulfment of this man who was the center of his life. He moved toward Rickey, stopped, made himself roll over on his back again. What was he doing? You didn't wake up a concussion victim who'd just had a night from hell because you were horny.

He reached down and cupped his balls with one hand, grabbed his dick with the other and squeezed the head so hard that he gave an involuntary little grunt of pain.

"G, what are you doing?"

"Nothing."

"You jerking off?"

"Kinda."

"Is there some particular reason you'd lay there yanking your crank instead of just waking me up?"

"Well...I figured you needed your rest."

Rickey snorted. "I couldn't sleep anyway with all that whispering, you old Holy Joe."

"Sorry. I just couldn't quit thinking—"

Rickey stopped his mouth with a kiss, palmed his dick and stroked, squeezed, stroked, mustering the expertise and affection G-man had been unable to summon. G-man wrapped his arms around Rickey's neck, careful to keep away from the knot on the back of Rickey's head.

And just like that, life was good again. There was no pall of fear, no blinding rage. He felt effortless tears on his cheeks. Rickey wasn't bothered; he just rubbed his face against G-man's, wetting them both further. One of Rickey's unspoken erotic mottoes was *the more bodily fluids, the better;* he loved the taste and feel of come, sweat, spit, tears. He also liked to talk a lot; they both did, the meaningless call and response of love: *you like that, you want some more, yeah, oh, give me it, please give me it.* Their tastes were simple and similar and, sixteen years after that first kiss, as happily pedestrian as those of any old married couple.

Sex had almost always been able to fix things for them, whether tension between themselves or the depredations of the world at large. It was never complicated, never something they used as a tool or a bargaining chip, nor lost the knack of even on the rare occasions when something else was off-kilter between them. G-man didn't know if other couples were this lucky, but for their sake, he hoped so. The inextricable blend of friendship, passion, and soul-deep comfort with Rickey was by far the sweetest gift the world had ever given him. He couldn't imagine what life would be like without it; he suspected that without it there might well be no life.

SHAKE MOVES UP IN THE WORLD

Shake Vojtaskovic was deeply and secretly ashamed of the fact that when he got promoted to head chef of La Pharmacie, his first thought was *This is really gonna put the piss in Rickey's cornflakes.*

There was no reason for such a flash of pettiness. He'd worked with Rickey for more than a decade, off and on. Rickey wasn't always easy to get along with— hell, let's face it, Rickey wasn't *usually* easy to get along with—but Shake genuinely liked the guy. He was funny, insanely talented, basically good-hearted. There was just something about him that set your nerves on edge, that put tinfoil between your teeth, that made you think about pissing in his cornflakes.

Of course there was also the fact that Rickey had originally worked under him—Shake had been sous chef at the Peychaud Grill when Rickey and G-man were raw line cooks—and he had ended up working under Rickey, but that was no big deal. Rickey had hit the jackpot three years ago with one genius idea (a menu based entirely on booze) and financial backing from celebrity chef Lenny Duveteaux. Shake was more of a journeyman cook, fast and solid but not long on ambition. Though he'd been cooking since he was seventeen, this was the first head chef job he'd ever held, and he had only gotten it by way of a horrible accident.

Chef Götz LaVey took inordinate pride in his long, luxurious blond hair; he claimed it was a chick magnet equivalent to if not greater than a badass car, a fat bank account, or a huge dick (which he also claimed to possess, not that anybody wanted to know about that). He wore it pulled back in a ponytail when he was cooking, of course, but that hadn't helped him on the day the automatic meat slicer jammed while cutting the beef daube glacé. If anything, the 'do had made it easier for the machine to yank his face into the gleaming machinery when the thing kicked back on as he was examining it. Individual strands of hair might have ripped out of his scalp, but the ponytail reeled him in like a bull redfish. During his twenty-one years in restaurant kitchens, Shake had grated his knuckles, sliced through his nails, amputated his fingertips, worked with hangovers and the stomach flu, and smelled chicken that had been rotting in a powerless walk-in cooler for two weeks, but he was proud of the fact that he'd never puked on the job...until the day of the daube glacé. There was no shame in it, though; everybody in the kitchen had puked that day.

Chef Götz wasn't incapacitated for long, but he would need plastic surgery and skin grafts. Worse, he'd turned blade-shy; word was he couldn't even touch a paring knife. The head chef job was Shake's by default, starting that night.

La Pharmacie achieved its trendiness by unearthing ancient Creole dishes and replicating them with a twist, often an ill-advised one; Götz had been planning to serve the daube glacé with pineapple-Tabasco crème fraîche and Indian fry-bread. After he rode off in the ambulance, Shake pried the big jellied hunk of beef and aspic out of the slicer, washed off the blood, pared away the portions that had come in closest contact with Götz's rearranged physiognomy, and sliced it by hand. It didn't come out as paper-thin as it would have in the slicer, but then again, Shake still had both cheekbones and all of his nose. He trashed the crème fraîche and Indian frybread, sent the pantry bitch out for several boxes of Melba toast, and served the daube with a garlic horseradish cream. It was the bestselling app they'd had in weeks. La Pharmacie's owners started thinking maybe Götz should have made an appointment with the meat slicer ages ago.

Today, with Götz's mishap a few weeks in the past, *Big Easy* magazine had sent a photographer over to take Shake's picture for a feature on new chefs at old restaurants. Less than a year in business, La Pharmacie didn't qualify as an "old" restaurant by any standards, let alone New Orleans ones whereby any restaurant open for under two decades was considered a young upstart. Shake guessed there hadn't been much top-end turnover at Antoine's, Arnaud's, or Broussard's lately. He didn't mind having his picture made, but the photographer had left him a few back issues of the magazine, and as Shake flipped through it while eating his staff meal, he reflected that he didn't think he had ever seen an issue of *Big Easy* without a picture of Rickey in it. If it was possible to receive blowjobs from a magazine, *Big Easy* would put G-man out of business. Rickey had been on the cover twice already, once when they'd named him Chef of the Year and once when Liquor had won a James Beard award. Not that he didn't deserve it—he'd blown away most of his competition for the local honor, and a Beard award was a huge deal in the food world—but Shake couldn't help wondering whether Rickey would have made the cover both times if he'd looked like, say, Danny DeVito. Maybe so; God knew Lenny Duveteaux was no looker, and he'd probably been on more *Big Easy* covers than any other chef in history.

The picture Shake was looking at now showed both of Liquor's co-chefs at the top of a story about The New Cocktail Culture, whatever the hell that was. Both were dressed in their whites. Rickey sat at a table holding a glass of what could have been any kind of whiskey, but Shake knew it was Wild Turkey. That and beer were about the only things Rickey ever drank. His hair was a lot shorter than it had been the last time Shake had seen him, almost buzzed. His vivid eyes, more turquoise than strictly blue, blazed out of the photograph. Rickey was not a skinny guy by anybody's standards, but there was a sharp, nervous cast to his features that the camera loved. G-man stood behind him, tall and rangy, arms folded across his chest. He had removed his shades for the photograph, but Shake thought he should have kept them on; his squint and his long, blunt nose gave him a moleish look.

"Cocktails are a way of celebrating different cultures," Rickey was quoted as saying. "Look at how the Sazerac symbolizes New Orleans, how the daiquiri makes you think of pre-Communist Cuba. It's a little bit of somebody's world, right there in your glass." Shake knew Rickey loathed Sazeracs and thought any mixed drink with more than two ingredients was "floofy." He wondered if he, too, would have to become fluent in Media Bullshit now that he was a head chef. Maybe he should call Rickey, get some pointers.

He thought he'd done all right, though. He wondered if he'd hear from Rickey when the issue featuring him came out. Shake had always believed in giving credit where credit was due, and this interview had been no exception.

STANK-ASS MOTHERFUCKER

G-man could usually tell whether or not it was going to be a good mail day by the look on Karl's face when he handed over the mail. Karl was the maître d', and he knew Rickey's moods as well as anyone in the front of the house. Bills were neutral, a fact of life. Personal letters were bad, as they usually indicated a customer who'd been unhappy enough with some aspect of his meal to pen an impassioned screed about it. Food and trade magazines could go either way—Rickey liked looking at them, but generally found something in them to piss him off. Today's mail looked iffy: a hand-addressed letter from something called Ducks Unlimited, probably a financial solicitation, and the new issue of *Big Easy*.

Rickey was in the office making out next week's schedule. G-man dropped the letter on his desk and started paging through the copy of *Big Easy*. This didn't look good. A feature on new chefs at old restaurants quoted Shake Vojtaskovic, late of Liquor and currently of La Pharmacie, saying, "If I've learned anything from my last few jobs, it's to avoid the gimmick. Don't go for a cute trick or an easy sell. Just make good, simple food—that's what diners really want."

G-man must have made some small sound in his throat, because Rickey looked up, saw the expression on his face, and snatched the magazine out of his hands. He read silently, his lips moving. For a moment G-man dared to think maybe there wouldn't be an explosion. Then it came: "GIMMICK? GIMMICK? I'LL GIVE HIM 'AVOID THE GIMMICK'!" Rickey grabbed the phone. G-man hoped Shake wouldn't be at the restaurant, but it was no good; Rickey knew Shake's cell number.

A torrent of invective such as G-man had seldom heard, even from his notoriously foul-mouthed partner, came pouring out as soon as Shake picked up. "Gimmick? GIMMICK? You stank-ass motherfucker! You shit-sucking bitch, I'll give you a gimmick right up your wide tan track! You got such a problem with my gimmick, how come I never heard nothing about it when you was working here, making goddamn good money too, you motherfucking bitch-ass cracker—" At his angriest, Rickey tended to revert to a Lower Ninth Ward street patois that was somewhere between black and yat.

"Rickey," G-man could hear Shake saying on the other end. "Rickey, listen."

"Yeah, listen to my ass in your face, you fucking shit-stain—"

"Rickey—"

"Give him a chance," G-man murmured.

"What," Rickey said finally. It was not a question; nor was there any hint of open-mindedness in it. Rickey was sensitive about his gimmick, always had been.

"Look," said Shake, and G-man reached across Rickey to punch the button that would put him on speakerphone; he wanted to hear this. "I know it sounds like I was talking about Liquor, but I swear to God, they took my shit out of context. I was talking about the stupid-ass gimmicks of the guy who was chef here before me. You know he was gonna serve beef daube glacé with pineapple-Tabasco créme fraîche?"

Rickey was stunned into silence, but only for a moment. Then he glanced back down at the article and said, "Yeah, so what's this shit about your *last few jobs?* Seems to me working here was one of your *last few jobs.*"

"Well..."

"Yeah. That's pretty much what I thought."

"It was just the damn liquor all the time!" Shake cried, real desperation in his voice. "I think you're a hell of a chef, Rickey, and Liquor's a great restaurant. But god-DAMN, don't you ever get tired of having to find a way to stick booze in everything?"

"Booze set me free," Rickey said, and now his voice was not ghetto-raw, but icy. "Booze gave me a way to have my own restaurant with G, and cook the food I want to cook, and you better fucking believe I'm not sick of it. What I'm sick of is cooks who make their reputations here, then get a job in some trendy shithole and take a dump on us the first chance they get."

"Hey, I didn't make my *reputation* at Liquor. In case you forgot, I was sous chef at the Peychaud when you were one of Paco's little line bitches."

"Oh, right, and the name Shake Vojtaskovic was on the lips of culinary New Orleans. I guess I did forget. You know damn well the only cook that mattered at the Peychaud was Paco himself."

"Yeah, yeah, Paco Valdeon, a.k.a. God. I hadn't known Paco better, I'd a thought maybe you and him had a thing going on, the way you talk about him."

"WHAT? LISTEN, YOU CAN SUCK MY HAIRY NUTSACK, YOU FUCKING WAD OF FUCKJUICE—"

G-man plucked the receiver out of Rickey's hand, leaving Rickey to gawp at him in utter, frozen surprise. He put the phone to his own ear and said, "You know what, Shake? That was low even for you. But guess what? We forgive you, because you got no idea what you're getting into taking over that place, and the shit you'll be dealing with is gonna be worse than your wildest dreams."

Gently, he replaced the receiver in its cradle. For a minute he and Rickey just stared at each other. Then Rickey said, "Well, I think you handled that better than I did."

G-man laughed. After a moment, reluctantly, Rickey did too.

"Fuck him," said G-man. "It's his first head chef job, he thinks he's hot shit, that's all. He'll be Flavor of the Month for a little while and then everybody'll move on to some other trendy joint. People might laugh at our gimmick, but we got staying power."

"Yeah, cause New Orleanians like to get drunk."

"It's not just that and you know it. Here, open the rest of your mail."

"Just junk," Rickey muttered. He picked up the envelope from Ducks Unlimited and slit it open with an old paring knife. As he read, his eyes grew wide and the scowl left his face. When he had finished, he handed the letter to G-man.

> Dear Chef John Rickey:
>
> I am writing to you as a representative of Ducks Unlimited. As you may know, we are a major conservation organization dedicated to the preservation of wetlands and other waterfowl habitats. We are currently planning our annual banquet for 300 members to be held on December 14 at the Delta Grand, a historic theater in downtown Opelousas, which has a banquet space and a full cafeteria-style kitchen. We will have a number of guest speakers including our Guest of Honor, avid sportsman, bona fide Cajun, and former New Orleans Saints quarterback Bobby Hebert. We are interested in having you and your crew prepare the banquet as we

want to do something a little different this year. We plan to have every course feature wild duck shot in Louisiana, and we understand that you are an expert at planning gourmet menus based around one ingredient. If interested, please contact me with a quote for the meal.

Sincerely yours,

Aristide "Tee" Fontenot
President, Ducks Unlimited,
St. Landry Parish Chapter

VII

SEPTEMBER 14, 1986

John Randolph Rickey had turned thirteen eight days ago, and everybody knew thirteen was the age when you were really, for true, no-bullshit grown up. Even his mother agreed with him: convinced that pro football games were venues of peril and iniquity, Brenda had banned her son, a rabid Saints fan, from ever attending one. When he argued—which he frequently did—she laid the blame on his father. "If Oskar was here, babe, he could take you. That's a father's place. That Dome ain't no place for me."

"But Gary's dad could take us, or Little Elmer, Carl..." There was a variety of Stubbs sons old enough to accompany a pair of kids to a football game.

"No, I ain't gonna impose on them for your mortal responsibility. You over there enough as it is. Poor Mary Rose probably thinks she got her seven kids instead of six."

In fact, Mary Rose Stubbs had welcomed Rickey into her home since the boys had become inseparable at nine. Rickey wondered whether she'd keep doing so if she knew some of the weird thoughts he'd been having about her youngest son lately; she was a pretty strict Catholic. He doubted, though, that she would have any qualms about assuming his "mortal responsibility" for a couple of hours.

But none of that was at issue now. What mattered to Rickey was that, for reasons known only to herself, his mother had decided that thirteen was old enough for a boy—a young man, she'd called him—to attend a football game in the presence of someone other than his father. She had even bought his ticket, or at least arranged it somehow with Elmer Stubbs, who knew a guy in the ticket office. Rickey had been watching the Saints on TV ever since he could remember, but today he would see them in person, playing the Green Bay Packers.

The Saints really stank. Rickey wasn't a big enough fan to deny that; some of the longtime fans almost seemed to take a perverse pride in it. In 1980, they had won a single game and lost fifteen. Local TV sportscaster Buddy Diliberto started wearing a paper bag over his head on the air, and fans followed suit. The next couple of seasons weren't much better. In 1983 they finally went 8-8, tying their previous record. The next two seasons slid downhill again, but this year the owner had hired a new coach, and last year's rookie quarterback had looked good in the preseason. The fans were hopeful in their fatalistic way.

Rickey had particular hopes for the quarterback, Bobby Hebert. He was a Louisiana boy: an actual Cajun from Cut Off, a wide spot on the bayou two hours south of New Orleans. Rickey had followed Hebert's career since his college days at Northwestern Louisiana, where he'd been a record-setter and got drafted into the USFL after his senior year. He'd hoped to go right into the NFL, but with a wife, a baby daughter, and food stamps buying the groceries, he couldn't afford to wait around and see if the more glamorous league would give him a whirl. He signed with the Michigan Panthers, made a nice chunk of change, and earned the nickname "The Cajun Cannon" with eighty-one touchdowns, more than 3500 yards per season, and two trips to the USFL championships.

In 1985, he became a free agent and it was a given that he'd enter the NFL. Everyone expected him to sign with the Seahawks until a senator in Cajun country decided that if a native son was going to play in the *real* pros, he should do it on Louisiana soil. The senator called the governor, Edwin Edwards, who was a Cajun too. The governor called the quarterback and said, "Hey, coonass, how come you tryin to go to Seattle? I hear it rains all the time out there and they got no food you'd wanna eat." And then Edwards set up a meeting with Saints owner Tom Benson, and Bobby Hebert came home to play.

Rickey loved this story. He'd grown up with poor kids who dreamed of making their fortunes as sports stars; it was his generation's version of a fairy tale. Even more than that, it was the food stamps. He and Brenda were no strangers to the envelope in the purse, the non-food items sorted into a separate pile on the conveyer belt, the occasional roll of the eyes from a wealthier shopper who'd made a pit stop at the ghetto Schwegmann's. Sure, Bobby Hebert was rich now...but even so, it must have taken guts to say right out loud to a newspaper reporter that he'd had to feed his family with food stamps.

Also, he was pretty good-looking. Rickey didn't give that more weight than it deserved, but it didn't hurt, either.

Gary Francis Stubbs—not yet known as G-man; that badge of honor would be awarded him six years later by the most foul-mouthed chef he ever worked under—had turned thirteen in July and didn't think it was such a big deal. Rickey was an only child. When you had five brothers and sisters all older than you, thirteen didn't seem like such a lofty age; there was always somebody around to remind you that you didn't know anything yet. He'd also been to several Saints games. But this was the first one he'd ever been to with Rickey, and he was excited about that. His weird thoughts about Rickey lately had been very much like the ones Rickey had had about him, though, still fairly deep in the thrall of the Church, Gary hadn't given these thoughts free rein or even truly allowed them into his conscious mind. More than that, he simply *enjoyed* Rickey, always had. Everything was a lot more fun and interesting with Rickey around. To Gary, whose lifelong bad vision frequently caused him to think in optic terms, it was as if Rickey brought things into focus.

"You boys want a hot dog or anything?" said Elmer Stubbs. He was a lanky, sweet-natured man who closely resembled his son in looks and demeanor. They already had drinks, a vast beer for Elmer, another discreetly poured into two empty cups for the boys. Rickey had known how to drink beer for a couple of years and was just beginning to dabble in liquor, with mixed results. Gary, like most children of Sicilian blood, had been drinking red wine with dinner since he was weaned. Besides, Elmer said a man couldn't watch a football game without a beer to drink; to hear him tell it, this was practically the law.

"Nah, Daddy, let's get to our seats. We can grab something at the half."

They followed an usher's pointing hand, descended a short flight of concrete steps, and emerged into the most amazing space Rickey had ever seen. He'd known the Superdome was big. You could see that much from the outside, and he knew the stats, of course: it covered fifty-two acres; it was the largest domed building in the world. But that didn't communicate an iota of what happened to your brain when you entered the part of the building that held the seats, the field, the tremendous overarching dome itself. Rickey had never been in any of the world's great cathedrals save St. Louis in Jackson Square, and then only on a school field trip where he'd idly wondered whether God would strike him dead if he palmed the five-dollar bill he could see poking out of the metal box where tourists stuck them before lighting candles. (Ultimately, more out of loyalty to Mary Rose than God, he hadn't.) Because he was not subject to religious awe, it was doubtful that any cathedral could have affected him as did this mind-assaulting expanse of bleachers and rafters and great translucent roof, ersatz sky glowing like neither day nor night. He felt a little dizzy. With the hand that was not holding his half-cup of beer, he grabbed a railing and wrapped his fingers tightly around it. For a moment it seemed to be all that tethered him to the concrete floor, that kept him from falling up, somehow, into the infinite moonscape of the Dome. Then he got a grip on himself and was fine.

"Don't worry," Elmer said. "We don't got sideline seats or nothing, but we ain't in the nosebleed section either. It's just down this way a little."

To Rickey, the seats seemed very close to the field, and he was enraptured from the coin toss on. The Saints scored a touchdown just a minute and a half into the game, and on the next drive, Bobby Hebert threw an eighty-four-yard pass to wide receiver Eric Martin. Rickey had understood the nickname "Cajun Cannon" in a theoretical way, but when he saw that ball leave Hebert's grasp and sail more than half the length of the field, moving so hard and fast that it seemed to bludgeon its way through the air, he realized for the first time that some people were simply designed to do a thing well. If they got to do it, then the world was a little better. It was the closest he had ever come to believing in any form of divine creation.

Hebert's bomb took the ball to the Packers' seven-yard line and set up an easy field goal for kicker Morten Anderson. Things sort of went downhill after that—the offense fell apart as it was apt to do, Bobby Hebert threw a couple of interceptions, and the defense had to mop up the mess—but the Saints won the game 24-10. By the time they filed out of the Dome, ascending those impossible levels among crowds of grinning, chattering fans dressed in black and gold, Rickey was euphoric, a little drunk on his second half-beer, and completely hooked. If someone had told him then and there that he'd just inherited a million dollars, his first splurge would have been a pair of season tickets. No, a trio, so Elmer could buy them beer. Elmer was absolutely right about the beer.

On the way home, in the backseat of Elmer's old rattletrap Pontiac, Rickey wondered if he would ever do anything as well as Bobby Hebert had thrown that eighty-four-yard bomb. He must have been put on earth to do something; certainly he had never felt purposeless. But what was his purpose? What talent lay buried in him that he didn't know about yet? Because he was not a reflective person by nature, this line of thought made him vaguely uneasy. He wished the talent would hurry up and show itself. On the heels of that thought, he wondered what Mary Rose was cooking tonight; he had been invited to stay for dinner and she was a wonderful cook.

"Hey, Daddy, I think Rickey's drunk," Gary said.

"Now don't you go telling your momma I bought you boys beer."

"Look at him, he's falling asleep. You damn waste case."

"Language," Elmer said automatically, but it was just something Mary Rose had drilled into him; he didn't really care if they cussed.

"I'm not drunk," Rickey said. "I'm thinking about the game."

"You're wasted on one beer. You got red eyes like a old stewbum."

Rickey roused himself from his daze to crawl across the seat and knuckle Gary's head, and Gary grabbed his arm, and they wrestled in the vast backseat while Elmer piloted them safely home. The beer was still pleasantly muzzy in his head, the sensation of his best friend's skin on his own was delicious in a presexual way, and all in all, Rickey reflected then and later—even years later—that had probably been one of the finest days of his life.

VIII

DUCK

O f course, his purpose and his talent turned out to be cooking. He'd started to realize that a year or so later, when he began to experiment with recipes from the cookbooks his mother bought but seldom used. When they were fifteen, he and G-man had gotten their first restaurant jobs as dishwashers at a Lower Ninth Ward greasy spoon, where Rickey eventually pestered the owner into letting them work the grill.

The thought that he might now design an elaborate meal for Bobby Hebert, who had first put into his head the whole idea of purposes and talents, overwhelmed him completely. The quarterback had long since retired and was now hosting a local sports talk radio show, but as far as Rickey was concerned, he was the biggest star Louisiana had ever produced. Still good-looking, too—better, probably, with a wash of silver in his black hair and perfect new teeth to replace the ones knocked out in Tampa Bay and all the other smashmouth games. The Cannon hadn't been one of those quarterbacks who danced around the action; he had always played hard, hard.

G-man saw all this going through Rickey's head and pointed at the letter. "Look. See there? Banquet for three hundred.

That means steam-table splooge. Quit picturing yourself swanning around some cute little private dining room serving perfect dishes to Bobby Hebert."

"It wouldn't have to be splooge. We could find a way to do it right."

"We can find a way to do something they'll love, sure. I'm not saying we shouldn't do it. I just want you to give up the idea of being Bobby Hebert's personal chef."

"I'm not…" For the first time since he'd opened it, Rickey looked up from the letter, saw G-man's face and G-man's absolute knowledge of him. Suddenly embarrassed, he laid the letter facedown on the desk. "Hell. I dunno. Maybe we shouldn't do it. Liquor, beef, now duck—I'm sick of people thinking I'm some kinda one-trick whore."

"Pony."

"Pony, hell. People get the idea you do one thing well and ask you to do it over and over again, they think you're a whore, not a damn pony."

Looking at Rickey, G-man remembered a dream he'd had a few nights ago. In it, he was the same broke-ass Lower Ninth Ward boy he'd always been, but Rickey was the scion of some rich family, the kind of kid who might have been an escort at the Rex ball. Oddly, this vast imaginary gulf in their social status had made their budding relationship not more difficult but easier; no one suspected, whereas in real life their folks had pegged it almost immediately because the two families lived just a few blocks apart and saw each other all the time. (Despite this proximity, Rickey *could* have put on airs about his neighborhood if he'd wanted to. He had grown up in the subsection closer to the river known as Holy Cross, while the Stubbses lived on the other side of St. Claude Avenue and were plain old Lower Ninth Warders.) They had thought they were being terribly secretive, but it's hard to be secretive when you are sixteen and in the throes of either true love or desperate lust; the combination makes it wholly impossible. In G-man's dream, rather than their hungry bouts of after-school sex where and when they could get them, they had been able to spend entire greedy nights in Rickey's huge Uptown house, in his bedroom far away from the rest of his sketchy dream-family, wallowing in it the way they really had done when they first moved in together. Nineteen, with nothing but a few crappy pots and pans and an old double bed G-man's sister Rosalie had given them. They'd worn out the bed within a year, though it had had to serve them two more.

G-man wondered now whether the dream could have had something to do with how their life had actually turned out. Rickey wasn't an old-family scion, but his ideas and his ability to seduce people's palates had brought them, if not exactly fame and fortune, at least a lot more attention and cash than they'd ever expected to have. More than G-man had expected, anyway. He sometimes wondered if Rickey hadn't known all along, at the bottom of his mind, that he was going to build an interesting life for the two of them. They had a better bed, if not quite as much time as they'd like to wallow in it. And, of course, they did live Uptown now. People they knew from the Lower Ninth Ward still made a certain face sometimes upon learning of it, a kind of contemptuous wince. In the minds of some lifelong downtowners, anyone who lived Uptown was white, rich, racist, and probably a crook.

Without Rickey, G-man knew perfectly well, he would be a rock-solid line cook or sous chef in somebody else's restaurant. He would never have been head chef—would have deliberately avoided it—and he might not have started cooking at all, might have gotten a job at the candy factory where his father and his brother Henry worked. Now, because of Rickey, they got their pictures in magazines. They had been on TV once, interviewed by the lady from *Steppin' Out*. And, G-man had known as soon as he read the letter, now they would get a chance to travel. Opelousas was just three hours away, but to G-man, who had only gone farther than the Mississippi Gulf coast thrice in his life, it seemed a whole different world. It was the hometown of Louisiana's first celebrity chef, Paul Prudhomme, who had invented a dish so popular that it endangered an entire species of fish. There were black people there who played zydeco music on accordions and washboards. The police chief was always making the news for conducting war games (he called them "Homeland Security drills") without warning anybody first. G-man couldn't imagine what kind of place it would be, but he could hardly wait to get a look at it.

He occasionally wished Rickey liked to travel more. They could have gone to food shows and guest-chef appearances in Chicago, Napa, even France—all sorts of places, but Rickey said they wouldn't have a chance to see anything because they'd be too busy acting like trained seals. That might or might not be true, but G-man knew the real reason they hadn't accepted any of the invitations was because Rickey purely hated to leave New Orleans. He was like a little old man already, the way he had to be pried out of his natural element. He wouldn't even be considering the Ducks Unlimited gig if not for the promised presence of Bobby Hebert.

"You're not a one-trick pony or a whore either," he said. "You're a damn good chef who knows what Louisiana people like. We got people come from all over the state to eat at Liquor. We'll just take it to them for a change. Hell, you know what? Bobby Hebert's probably *already* eaten here."

"No he hasn't."

"How do you know?"

Rickey looked back down at the desk, and G-man thought he was blushing a little. "Cause when he took the WWL gig, I told Karl to come tell me right away if he ever came in, and if it was our night off, to call me."

"Oh." G-man thought about this for a moment, but it didn't really surprise him. "Well, anyway, come on, be serious. Of course we're gonna do it. How many cooks ever get the chance to cook a whole dinner using wild ducks?"

"What're we gonna do for the dessert?"

They looked at each other and suddenly grinned, because it was such a silly question. Tanker would take great pleasure in concocting a dessert that involved duck cracklins or a triangle of candied duck skin or some other crazy thing. It would sound disgusting and be delicious. Those were the kinds of dishes he lived for.

"You know what else?" Rickey said.

"What?"

"This'll put a fucking knot in Shake's panties."

Privately, G-man wondered: even with Bobby Hebert and a semi-famous chef, how much press was a Ducks Unlimited banquet in Opelousas likely to get here in New Orleans? If Rickey wanted to think so, though, there was no reason to argue. Some of Rickey's best ideas came as the result of vendettas.

LIKE A RAT IN THE WALL

The thing was—and Rickey hadn't even figured this out completely in his own mind, let alone spoken of it to G-man—that he was sick of being the kind of person who thrived on rages and vendettas. It was the cliché of the temperamental chef, the fat tyrant screaming in the kitchen. He wasn't much of a screamer, but plenty of his employees were scared of him and all were cautious around him. That part he liked; you couldn't run a restaurant right if your employees weren't a little scared of getting reamed out by you. It was the effect on the rest of his life that he didn't like so much. Last year, during a bout of back trouble, he'd had his first physical in years and learned that his blood pressure was high. Not dangerously high, but high for a guy in his early thirties who got a lot of physical activity. He didn't put much faith in doctors and only thought of it at odd moments, but he wondered if it was something he should be worried about.

Worse than the mystifying prognostications of doctors was the gnawing he felt inside himself, every day, almost every single minute of his life. It was like a rat gnawing in the wall of an old house, scraping ceaselessly at the punky wood until you thought the noise would drive you crazy and you started pounding on the wall. Lower Ninth Ward rats didn't always run away when you pounded, either. Rickey knew those rats well, and it seemed that one had moved Uptown with him, had taken up residence in his head, always there, doing its thing. The only times he didn't feel it were when he was sleeping, drunk, or having sex. G-man could ease it by talking to him sometimes, but even G-man couldn't make it go away entirely.

The conversation with Shake had woken the rat up good; it was fairly spinning in there. He'd think about it all night during service, replaying it in his mind, imagining how he could have given it to Shake even worse. God, he was so sick of that. He wanted to find a peaceful place within himself, the kind of place that G-man just seemed to have naturally. He'd asked G-man about it many times, but G-man didn't really know why he was the way he was; couldn't know; it was like asking him why he had chestnut-brown eyes when all his brothers' and sisters' eyes were nearly black. At best, he might say something about the steadiness of his favorite basketball players, Kareem Abdul-Jabbar, Karl Malone, Michael Jordan or some other mighty, unflappable hoopster. He drew strength from these things, and from whatever his belief in God meant to him. Rickey could not profit from such things. But maybe, if he were to cook a great meal for Bobby Hebert, who in a way had helped show him his purpose…

Christ, he was putting too much into the thing. At this rate he'd give himself a nervous breakdown before he even figured out the amuse-bouche.

So he pulled himself together and finished his prep work, and thankfully it was a busy night and he was able to lose himself in the rush during service. The next morning he got up early, called Aristide "Tee" Fontenot, talked over the details of the event, and offered a price that Fontenot accepted immediately. Rickey wondered if he should have gone higher, but he didn't really care; the price he'd named would net them a decent profit, and the presence of Bobby Hebert would be an immeasurable bonus. With hours left before he had to be at the restaurant, he started going through his cookbook collection. It had gotten a lot bigger over the past few years, since he'd had a little money, but for this he went to his old, well-thumbed, stained standards: Richard Olney, Elizabeth David, M.F.K. Fisher. Olney's *French Menu Cookbook* was his favorite cookery volume of all time, but it was no help here. Olney only dealt in foie gras, which of course they wouldn't have unless "Tee" Fontenot was willing to somehow catch a flock of wild ducks alive, keep them in a pen, and force-feed them twice a day until the banquet. His Elizabeth David omnibus was more useful. She had a great-sounding duck dish with cherries that Rickey was amused to realize his old friend and nemesis, the late celebrity chef Cooper Stark, had blatantly ripped off for his own cookbook. She also had duck in daube, which could be prepared ahead. In his mind's eye, Rickey saw it on a plain white plate—none of this holed, weird-colored, boomerang-shaped business for him—the translucent golden-brown aspic glistening, the duck meat subtly flecked with red and black pepper. Old-school. Confit could be done ahead, too, another good classic dish. They'd do both of those for sure.

Prepared ahead. Rickey scowled. How was that going to work? He picked up the phone and called Fontenot back. "Listen, Mr. Fontenot—"

"Aw, now none a' that. I awready told you, you gotta call me Tee."

"Tee," Rickey said with a little difficulty; in his mind it was a woman's name, one he associated with the old-line New Orleans restaurant Commander's Palace and the Brennan family. "Listen, what if I had some dishes I wanted to make ahead? Would you be able to get me some ducks in advance?"

"Like how many?"

Rickey thought about it. He could bone out the bodies and use them for the daube, keeping the wings and legs for the confit. He'd have to buy some duck fat—wild ducks were way too lean to make confit on their own—but that was OK. Two legs and two wings per duck, three hundred people...the servings would be small, of course. "Fifty?" he said.

Fontenot whistled. "Well, the season opens November 10. Birds runnin good, we might could get you fifty by the first of December. Some teal, pins, gadwalls, maybe a few dos gris if they early. Fly 'em into the city so they'll be nice and fresh. On a plane, I mean—their flyin days gonna be over!" Fontenot laughed heartily at his own joke.

Rickey thought about it. He'd been mostly lost after "teal," but had scrawled down phonetic approximations of the other names and would look them up on the Internet later. What mattered was the timing. Thirteen days, if the ducks arrived on time; a day to cut them up and do the preserving, so call it twelve; that would be just enough time for the confit to get good and seasoned. "I can work with that," he said.

"Good boy, good boy. Anything else I can help you with?" This was pronounced *Anyting else I kin help yoo wit?;* there was no -*th* sound in the Cajun accent.

"Not right now. I'll probably call you back about fifty times, though."

"You do that." *You doo dat.*

So: a cold amuse-bouche of duck en daube; then the confit with a nice vinaigrette salad, maybe arugula and frisée, sharp greens to cut the richness of the duck fat. But lots of people didn't like frisée. It could be tough, and it looked so ugly if it was even a little bit old. Bobby Hebert might not like it. Rickey had a nightmare vision of the Cajun Cannon fussily picking frisée out of his salad and setting it on the side of his plate. Red-leaf lettuce? It was tasteless, but it would look good with the dark green arugula. No! He had it: radicchio, slightly wilted in a little of the duck fat! It would be gorgeous *and* delicious.

So there was one, no, two dishes. Then a soup. They'd have to do a gumbo, of course; this crowd would probably string up the chef if they didn't get a gumbo. He didn't need a recipe for that; if he couldn't make a damn good duck and sausage gumbo after seventeen years in New Orleans kitchens, he might as well hang up his toque. He'd order some andouille from Poche's in Breaux Bridge…

But what if a damn good duck and sausage gumbo in New Orleans was only a mediocre one in Opelousas? Cajuns took their gumbo very seriously; their entire Mardi Gras celebration was based around it, or so Rickey, who'd never spent a Fat Tuesday outside of New Orleans, believed. Shit, he'd better do some research on that too.

G-man came into the kitchen rubbing his eyes, dressed in a pair of boxer shorts and a faded Utah Jazz T-shirt. "You're up early," he said.

"Ain't no jazz in Utah," Rickey answered. It was something he always said when he saw G-man wearing that particular T-shirt, and G-man paid it no more mind than he would if Rickey had said, "It's hot today." He wandered to the coffeemaker, poured himself a cup of the brew Rickey had fixed hours ago, tasted it, grimaced, and set about making a new pot.

When G-man finally had a cup of coffee in front of him, Rickey turned around the yellow legal pad he'd been making notes on and slid it across the table. G-man read his notes, frowning at the list of odd duck names—TEAL, PINS, GAT-WOLLS, DO GREE. "Aren't these dishes kinda labor-intensive for three hundred? I thought we'd just do your basic salad, gumbo, main course, dessert."

"Well, you thought wrong. I'm not doing some boring-ass banquet menu for these people. This is gonna be restaurant-quality food."

"You're not doing some boring-ass banquet menu for Bobby Hebert, you mean."

"No, I don't!" Rickey pulled his notebook back across the table. "Quit fucking teasing me about Bobby Hebert for one second. I'm not cranking out boring-ass banquet food for *any-body*. These people are paying good money and they want a fancy meal, the kinda shit they think we eat all the time in New Orleans. I'm damn well gonna give it to them."

"OK, OK." G-man's eyes suddenly looked more naked than usual, and Rickey felt bad for snapping at him.

"Sorry. I didn't mean to yell at you. I been up for hours—I probably need some more coffee." Rickey got up and poured himself a cup. "But seriously, G, I want to do this thing right. I'm not making splooge because I don't think that's what they want. I'm thinking more like a tasting menu, at least seven or eight courses."

"Fine. But where are you gonna get the crew?"

"We'll just close the restaurant for a couple days. Take the crew up there with us the day before the dinner, stay overnight, get into the hall early the next day and do all our prep."

G-man was shaking his head. "Rickey, what the fuck? We can't close the restaurant on a weekend right before Christmas. You know we're always busy then."

"This gig's paying well enough we can afford it. Hell, we could afford to stay over an extra night in Opelousas, see the sights."

"But you gotta consider the bad will it'll create. Walk-ins want dinner after they just spent all day Christmas shopping, find out we're closed—bang, they're pissed off, they're gonna cry and whine and tell the whole world about it."

"Fuck 'em," Rickey said stubbornly. "Let 'em go eat at La Pharmacie. That's the hot new place anyway, right?"

"Might not be by Christmas."

Rickey smiled, then scowled again. "Well, I don't care. That's what I was gonna do. If you really don't think we can close, we'll leave Terrance in charge of the kitchen with Marquis and Devonte. You, me, Tanker, and Jacolvy, we can knock out the dinner. I'm not one of these pussies who needs a crew of fifteen."

"Jacolvy? He doesn't know shit." Jacolvy was an eighteen-year-old Rickey had hired through a juvenile offenders' job training program. As a kid, he'd specialized in home burglaries and car robberies, and Rickey still kept a close eye on him around the kitchen equipment. He worked harder than any raw recruit Rickey had ever hired, though, and they had a soft spot for him because he'd grown up in the heart of the Lower Ninth Ward, on Tennessee Street right by the Industrial Canal levee.

"He'll be our prep bitch. Plus, by then, he'll know two more months' worth of shit than he does now."

G-man finished his coffee and got some more. On his face was a hangdog look that annoyed Rickey deeply. Finally he said, "What if I didn't do the dinner? You take everybody else with you. I'll stay and run the kitchen here by myself. I can do it for a couple nights if I had to, or maybe Lenny could lend me a cook."

"Fucking A! Run the kitchen by yourself, right. I thought if there was one person I never had to get into a dick-measuring contest with, it was you."

"I'm not trying to get into a dick-measuring contest. I just don't think we should close the restaurant and I don't think four cooks is enough to do a seven-course tasting menu for three hundred."

"Seven or eight courses," Rickey insisted. "A lot of the shit'll be prepped in advance—all we'll have to do is plate it up. I'd just as soon do this dinner without my knives as try to do it without you, and besides, I know you want to go to Opelousas."

It was true; Rickey could see it in G-man's face. *I never take him anywhere,* Rickey thought. But why *go* anywhere, when you got right down to it? Opelousas was fine; they could be back in New Orleans in three hours if need be. The thought of being more than three hours from New Orleans or unable to return to the city immediately for any reason filled Rickey with a deep and nameless dread. He supposed he wasn't very adventurous in some ways, but adventure outside of New Orleans had never worked out all that well for him. *Outside the city limits, the true heart of darkness begins.*

This adventure would work out well, though; he intended to make sure of it. He wasn't heading into the heart of darkness. He was cooking for Bobby Goddamn Hebert, and he'd be goddamned if G-man was going to kill his buzz.

Rickey turned to a fresh sheet of paper and dove back into his pile of cookbooks. G-man watched him for a moment, still worried but unable to keep himself from grinning a little. This fancy tasting-course plan sounded like the height of folly to him, but if Rickey was determined to make it happen, he probably would. After all, he had a winning track record.

NOT TO HAVE FIRE IS TO BE
A SKIN THAT SHRILLS

Shake finished leaving another irate message for his produce guy and hung up shaking his head. It was like people didn't hear what you told them, or simply didn't care. He had ordered pea tendrils and Sultan's Ruby heirloom tomatoes, specifically mentioning that he planned to combine them in a salad. It would have been an easy-ass dish for which he could charge $12 without anyone batting an eye. Unfortunately, he hadn't been here to inspect the order when it arrived yesterday, and the pea tendrils had made it but the tomatoes had not. Now the produce guy wouldn't return his calls. If he got the heirlooms today, he could still make the salad. After that, the pea tendrils would be past their prime and he'd have to use them in another dish. Maybe some sautéed Gulf fish with a vinaigrette sauce, like he'd seen Cole Parker doing over at Poivre.

Shake didn't have a lot of experience designing specials and was a little dismayed at the constant temptation to rip off other chefs, chefs who seemed to seemed to have their fingers on the pulse of the fine-dining crowd more firmly than he did. Well, if he paired the pea tendrils with the fish, he'd use morels instead of the oyster mushrooms Cole Parker was doing. *White* morels, if he could get them. Nobody in New Orleans was doing white morels.

"Hey, Shake?" said the manager, leaning familiarly through the pass. That was another problem—two, actually: nobody in the place called him Chef, and the front-of-the-house people felt far too comfortable in his kitchen. He'd never thought he would care about the former issue, but it turned out that when even the greenest pantry bitches forgot to address you as Chef, it affected the entire restaurant's perception of you. As for the latter, no chef wanted front people in his kitchen unless they were good-looking waitresses impressed by a white coat. Not that there had been much of that at Liquor, not under that tyrannical turquoise eye.

"Yeah, what?"

"The people from *Cornet* are here. They said you were supposed to do an interview and get your picture made for the fall dining guide."

"Aw, crap."

He'd begun to understand why Rickey sometimes seemed to have extreme tunnel vision: if you didn't tune out the distractions, you'd never get anything done. Publicity begat publicity, and there was always somebody wanting to take your picture, get a quote, jack you off. The only good part was that sometimes the handjobs were literal rather than figurative. Plenty of women really *did* lubricate at the sight of a white coat; he'd always taken advantage of that, but it was a lot easier to do so when you were the head chef.

That wouldn't be happening today, though, he reflected as the pair from the local freebie paper entered the kitchen. The writer was a plump little man with a long, snuffling nose and an unfortunate mustache. The photographer was a broad-shouldered woman with a buzz cut, an earring in the shape of a pink triangle, and a T-shirt that said **WHAT WAS YOUR FIRST CLUE?**

"Humphrey Wildblood," said the writer, extending a short-fingered hand. "We don't have much space—I've got to accommodate all the restaurants that advertise in *Cornet*—so I'll need you to boil down your philosophy of cooking to a sentence or two."

The photographer glanced around the kitchen. Her gaze settled on the six-burner flattop and the big sauté pans hanging above it. "Say," she said, "do you think you could set something on fire?"

"Uh, I'm not really cooking anything yet."

"Yes, but it would *look cool in the picture,*" she told him patiently, as if addressing an infant or someone who'd maybe won a silver medal in the Special Olympics.

"I don't know, Dymphna," said Humphrey Wildblood. "I always like those pictures where the chef's sitting at a table with a nice glass of wine."

Dymphna? thought Shake, but he knew when he was beaten. If his choices were the dreaded Wineglass Shot or setting something on fire, he'd take the option that made him look like a macho idiot over the one that made him look like a preening pussy.

As he poured cheap bourbon into an empty pan and tilted it so that the flames caught the liquor and billowed up like a special effect at a Kiss concert, Shake prayed that Rickey wouldn't see this picture. He knew there was little chance of getting his wish—every cook, waiter, and foodie in New Orleans looked at *Cornet*'s fall dining guide, if only to snark at Humphrey Wildblood's alternately acidic and ass-kissing descriptions—but every now and then the gods smiled. He had thought they were doing so when they dragged Götz into the meat slicer and gave him this job, but he was already beginning to wonder.

THE HELPING HAND

"**W**hat the hell is this thing?" G-man asked Jacolvy for the third time.

He'd entered the walk-in to find the kid rummaging surreptitiously among boxes and bins. At first he'd just hung back and watched, wondering if Jacolvy was going to steal a couple of steaks or a bag of shrimp. He hated thinking that way about his employees, but he and Rickey didn't have any prior experience with the juvenile offenders' training program and didn't know what to expect from an eighteen-year-old who'd already wreaked more havoc in the world than the two of them combined. However, it soon became apparent that Jacolvy was intent not on removing anything but on concealing something. That was when G-man cleared his throat and stepped forward. He wasn't entirely opposed to drugs on the premises, but if they were going to be there, he was damn sure going to know about them.

"Chef! I was just, uh, uh..."

G-man reached up and grabbed the item he'd seen Jacolvy drop behind a row of empty stock containers. It wasn't a dime bag of pot or a crack rock like he'd figured, but a small packet of black cloth wrapped in white thread. It gritted between his fingers as if some very dry, stemmy pot might be inside, but somehow he didn't think this was about drugs after all: there was something ceremonial-looking, even elegant about the little packet. "What is it?" he asked.

Jacolvy dodged the question. G-man asked him again, and he obfuscated. The third time G-man asked, though, the kid's shoulders sagged and he seemed to give up. "It's a toby. A helping hand. My momma give it to me. She made me promise to hide it here in the restaurant so I could keep my job."

"Keep your...?" A tingle ran through G-man's fingers. "Is this some kinda voodoo thing? I thought you were Catholic." G-man glanced down at Jacolvy's right forearm, thin but beginning to be ropy with the muscles you got from sautéing; there was a spark of talent in him, and they'd been letting him make a bunch of staff meals. "You got a rosary tattoo."

"I ain't nothin one way or the other. That's for my momma. See, it got her initials in the middle, DRT—Drylean Renee Turner. She's Spiritual."

"Spiritual?" Now G-man was completely baffled; as far as he knew, that was a kind of song people sang in black churches, but not a whole religion.

"African Spiritual church. She go to St. Anthony of Padua on Almonaster."

"Sounds Catholic to me."

"They like all them Catholic saints awright, and they pray to Jesus and say the rosary. It ain't no voodoo church like people think. They just do a little rootwork, little candle burnin. My momma, she take me to the Reverend, say she fraid I gonna get fired cause I missed one little old parole meetin. Reverend wrote my name a buncha times on a piece of paper, wrote the name of this restaurant, y'all's names."

"Me and Rickey?"

"Yeah. Then he taped 'em to the bottoms of candles and made me say prayers and eat pecan pie while he burned 'em."

"Pecan *pie?*" G-man was sure he couldn't have heard that last part right.

"Yeah. It wasn't as good as my grammaw's, but it was tollable." Now that G-man had made him start this story, Jacolvy seemed determined to finish it. "Then the Rev, he give me that there helping hand, say I gotta hide it here in the restaurant. Say I ain't gonna get fired long as I do my job and nobody find that thing."

"You're not gonna get fired if you do your job *anyway,*" G-man said. "You really believe this stuff?"

"I dunno, man." Jacolvy looked miserable, but defiant. "I heard Chef sayin you went to Mass one day. You really believe them priests turn wine into blood and all?"

"I don't take Communion anymore." But G-man saw the kid's point. "I don't know. I was raised with all that stuff."

"Well, you know how it is then." Jacolvy's thin face was miserable; G-man saw that his eyes, which had always had a hooded, closed-off look, now sparkled with ill-concealed tears. "Mostly I just done it for my momma. She so desperate to see me do right, keep a job, and I done messed up so much..." He shrugged helplessly. "I just thought maybe it make her believe in me, make her get some peace in her heart about me."

G-man felt a lump in his throat. If he didn't watch it, he was going to be back here bawling in the cooler with their young felon. He handed the little packet back to Jacolvy. "Just stick it up there on the shelf," he said. "Get it back in there good. We clean these lower shelves twice a month, but nobody ever cleans way back there." G-man started to turn away.

"Thanks, Chef." A pause, then: "Please don't tell Chef. He'd fire me for sure, I know it."

G-man looked back at him, more perplexed than ever. "Rickey wouldn't fire you for this. How come you think he would?"

"Cause he hates any kinda religious shit. I could tell by the way he said you went to Mass. I mean, he wasn't talkin trash about you or nothin, don't get the wrong idea, but..."

Jacolvy shrugged his thin shoulders expressively. With his slight build, huge brown eyes, and veneer of thuggishness over the soul of a man willing to get tattoos and do weird religious ceremonies for his momma, he was beginning to remind G-man of Allen Iverson, the NBA shooting guard who seemed to have ten pounds of heart for every pound of his body weight. Despite his scrapes with the law—hell, Iverson had had them too—G-man suddenly felt sure that Jacolvy was going to be a roller once he really learned his way around the kitchen.

"Well, Rickey isn't a big fan of organized religion, but he's not gonna fire you over it. That'd be illegal, for one thing."

"It would?" Jacolvy looked as amazed as if G-man had just told him he'd be expediting tonight.

"Sure, man. Didn't all those juvie courts and lawyers teach you anything?"

"Shhyeah. Taught me you better have a lotta fuckin money or the system gonna grind you down to a nub. I never met nobody in charge, black or white, who thought I was anything but trash till I got in the job trainin program."

"Shit. Well, I..." Now G-man was embarrassed, but he wasn't sure why. The awkward moment was broken by the sound of loud, maniacal laughter coming from the direction of Rickey's office.

"Jeez, I better go see what he's up to. Say, you wanna work an off-site banquet with us in December? You'd have to stay over a couple nights in Opelousas."

"I gotta check in with my PO, but yeah, sure, if she say I can."

"Let me know if you need us to talk to her," G-man said, and left Jacolvy to hide his helping hand in peace. As he hurried down the hall, he could hear Rickey pounding his fists on the desk, still laughing insanely.

"Dude. You finally just lost it, huh? I gotta stop what I'm doing and drive you down to the mental ward at Charity?"

Rickey looked up. The fall dining issue of *Cornet* was spread out on the desk before him. Wordlessly, he pointed to a picture. G-man walked around the desk and stood behind Rickey, leaning over to see what he'd gotten so worked up about. The picture showed a rather grim-looking Shake in chef's whites, his face almost obscured by the more photogenic tongues of fire shooting up from his pan. Beneath it, the caption read, "SNAKE VOJTASKOVIC of La Pharmacie is a flamer extraordinaire."

"Oh, *no,*" whispered G man, almost in awe. "They *didn't.*"

"They...they..." Rickey gulped, wiped his eyes. "They did."

"Flamer extraordinaire?" G-man bit the inside of his cheek, trying to maintain some sort of composure. His mother had taught him not to laugh at the misfortune of others.

"Snake," Rickey said, and set himself off again.

G-man couldn't help it; he started laughing. By the time he got himself under control, Rickey had picked up the phone and was dialing.

"Oh, you're not gonna—"

"Yeah, is this Chef Snake?" Rickey didn't pause to hear an answer, but plowed ahead. "I'm proud of you for finally taking one for the side. Look, you know I'm not really into the whole gay pride thing, but I think I got a rainbow flag around here somewhere. You can have it if you want to, you know, represent."

Rickey didn't have the speakerphone on this time, but G-man could still hear the resounding "FUCK YOU, RICKEY" and click of Shake ending the call.

G-man leaned against the wall, laughing so hard his stomach hurt. He slid slowly to the floor, grabbed a stray napkin from atop a nearby pile of cookbooks and magazines, and waved it in the air, surrendering. "Stop. I'm gonna die."

"So's Shake. I mean, Snake." In the worst faux-queeny voice G-man had ever heard, Rickey said, "Giiiiirrrrl, he's just gonna *die* of embarrassment."

G-man dropped the napkin and fell over on his side, legs kicking weakly in the air. If he didn't stop laughing soon, he thought he might actually pee himself.

"Rickey?" It was Tanker, standing at the office door. "Hey, Rickey, I need to—Jesus, what are you clowns *doing?*"

Rickey showed him the picture.

"Oh, no way," said Tanker. He looked again, laughed, and shook his head. "No fucking way. What, you got Humphrey Wildblood in your pocket now?"

"Course not," Rickey said with dignity. "I just got a pure heart and a damn good menu, and old Snake's starting to reap what the world owes him."

"You got a damn good menu," G-man said. "I don't know about the pure heart."

"Well, *you* got one anyway."

"Don't fuck with Chef Goodmenu and Chef Pureheart," said Tanker, rolling his eyes. "Instant karma gonna get you, gonna knock you off your feet."

"What feet? He crawls on his belly like a *rrrrreptile.*"

"Yeah, when he's not busy being a flamer extraordinaire."

"Oh my God," said G-man, picking up the napkin again and mopping his face with it. "Oh, jeez, please stop, I'm begging you."

By the beginning of service that night, the item had been cut out of the *Cornet,* taped carefully on the wall beside the expediting station, and pointed out to everyone who entered the kitchen. He might or might not make his proud mark on the world at large, but here at Liquor, Shake Vojtaskovic would never again be known by any other name than Snake the Flamer.

XII

THE WINE, THE MOONLIGHT, THE PROSCIUTTO

After closing the restaurant one night, Rickey and G-man drove out to a spot they liked on the shore of Lake Pontchartrain. They brought a bottle of wine—neither of them was much of a oenophile, but G-man was slowly working his way through the Italian reds, learning about better versions of what had always been on his family table—and sat on the seawall passing it back and forth, legs dangling above the surf, not talking much, watching the moonlight ripple on the dark unquiet water. It was October now, often one of the most beautiful months in New Orleans, but this had been a hot one and the breeze from the lake felt good on their slightly kitchen-baked faces.

As the level in the wine bottle decreased, they began to lean against each other. Eventually Rickey was leaning a little more, and G-man slipped an arm around his shoulders. They weren't much given to public displays of affection, but there was nobody else out here to see. Rickey let his head nestle into the curve of G-man's neck. His hair stank of sweat and grease, his skin was sticky, and there was a crusty stain on the sleeve of his T-shirt, but to G-man he felt wonderful.

"G?" Rickey said sleepily.

"Yeah, sweetheart?"

"You think fourteen days is enough to make a good duck prosciutto?"

G-man sighed.

"What?"

"Nothing. I just never thought I'd be jealous of a hundred ducks."

"Fifty ducks. Fifty is all we're getting in advance. Then around a hundred more when we get there, depending on how the season goes."

"Half a duck per person, huh?"

"Maybe a little more for Bobby Hebert."

"Can't we round it out with some city ducks?"

"Mr. Fontenot says they don't want any city ducks. What was it he called 'em?...Oh yeah. Marshmallows."

G-man laughed, then turned his head and put his lips against the soft hollow behind Rickey's ear.

"Mmmm...hey, listen..."

"Wha?" said G-man, muffled.

"What if we *wrapped* duck breasts in the prosciutto and...OW! Goddammit, G! Jesus Christ, you fucking *bit* me on the fucking *earlobe!* I can't believe it!"

"Sorry. I didn't mean to bite down like that."

"Do you want to go home or something?"

"I guess we can talk about ducks just as well here as there."

"We don't have to talk about ducks."

"You sure you can stop for five minutes?"

"I been a little single-minded, huh?"

"Yeah, like the Saints are having a little bit of a losing season...Aw, don't worry about it," he said to Rickey's wounded expression. "I know you gotta be single-minded about stuff like this. It's just, you know, it's only October."

"Exactly! It's way too early to say they're having a losing season. They could still go twelve and four."

"Sure they could, Mr. Who Dat, but I was talking about the banquet. You can't spend your every waking minute between now and December thinking about it. You still got a restaurant to run."

"Course I got a restaurant to run. But I *know* how to do that. I don't know how to do this banquet."

"We worked banquets before, back at Reilly's. And you done 'em at Escargot's."

"Yeah, but I never *planned* any. And besides, those were garbage. This one has to be perfect."

"Yeah, I know." It was no use reminding Rickey that things would inevitably fall short of perfection. Rickey knew that, but he still felt like a slacker if he didn't strive for perfection all the time and achieve it at least ninety percent of the time. It made him exhausting to work for. G-man didn't mind, as he was naturally a hard worker and found it easier to do things right than to go through the stress of fucking them up, but he admired the cooks who were able to remain a part of their crew for any length of time. Rickey really took it out of them, yet even the treacherous Shake had hung in there for three years. G-man knew Rickey was one of those head chefs who made the rest of the kitchen want to rise to his level. He also knew he could never have been such a chef himself; he had the talent and stamina, but not the drive or the ability to simultaneously terrify and inspire.

"Well, you wanna go home?"

"What for?" G-man said a bit sullenly.

"I don't know. Maybe take a shower, then get in bed and mess around?"

"I thought you didn't want to."

"Sure I want to. I'm just a little slow on the uptake."

"Well," said G-man. "Maybe." He wasn't really hedging; he just hoped Rickey would talk a little more about what they might do when they got home.

"Course, we don't have to wait till we get in bed to start messing around. Shower's big enough for two."

"Uh huh..."

"I just gotta look up this one duck galantine recipe first."

G-man had already knuckled the top of Rickey's head quite savagely before he saw that Rickey was laughing.

XIII

PARENTAL GUIDANCE SUGGESTED

Shake knew his family was coming in for dinner, but he hadn't expected their arrival to be heralded by his father's loud and unmelodious voice singing the jingle that had advertised the family's pest control business since 1953. "Don't let termites cave your WALL IN! Dial five two two six thousand, DAWLIN!"

A few minutes later the hostess ducked into the kitchen, a haunted look in her eye. "My God, Shake, your dad—I just asked him where I'd heard your family name before, because it's so unusual, and he started, like, *bellowing* at me—"

"I know," said Shake. "He's a little hard of hearing. Just make sure Orlando takes good care of them, huh?" Orlando was the only server over thirty at La Pharmacie, a career guy who gave the impression that he should certainly be making his fortune at Antoine's or Galatoire's, but had consented to slum among the tables of this flash-in-the-pan Uptown bistro. He was a prime asshole, but he was also the only waiter Shake trusted to handle the food right.

"Oh, of course, of course," she said, retreating gracefully. Bitch. She couldn't have lived in New Orleans long; else she'd know Vojtaskovic wasn't a particularly unusual name. A student, probably, studying business or pre-law or some damn thing. She was a bony creature with cropped hair, the kind of girl whose hipbones would bruise you as you fucked her, but she always looked at him as if certain he was dying to get into her tiny pink Capri pants. *Maybe if you stood in the pantry and dropped 'em,* Shake thought, *but I sure wouldn't go to any trouble over it.*

That was a terrible way to think about a woman, he knew, especially right before he went out to greet his own mother. Oh, God. What would she be wearing? He realized it had been at least ten years since he had seen her in anything besides the shapeless snap-fronted garments women her age called "house dresses." Trying to picture her sitting at one of La Pharmacie's sleek-varnished black tables in such a garment—maybe one with floral sprigs—he closed his eyes and shuddered a little.

He knew what his father would be wearing, anyway: a short-sleeved Oxford shirt, either solid blue or white with a blue stripe, and khaki pants hitched up a little too high. Since it was still warm, he would not be wearing his Saints windbreaker over the ensemble. Johnny Vojtaskovic hated the Saints now, but he had bought the jacket thirty years ago and was too cheap to buy another one as long as there was some life left in it.

Shake palmed sweat off his face, wiped his hands on a side towel, and went out to greet them. As he approached the table, he saw hopelessly that, although Lydia wasn't wearing one of her house dresses, the outfit she had chosen was almost as bad: some kind of brown skirt suit with a huge, pink, flagrantly artificial flower pinned smack in the center of the bosom. *Well, fuck it,* he thought as he bent down to kiss her, *just because I work in this fancy-ass joint now doesn't mean I gotta be ashamed of how my mom dresses.* He saw the hostess staring at them and gave her a look hard enough to make her busy herself among the menu folders.

"That girl didn't know who we were!" his father announced. "I hadda sing her the termite song!"

"I know, Dad. She's just a kid." Over his parents' heads, Shake met the eyes of his brother Rob, who'd come with his wife. Rob held down an administrative position at the Chalmette Refinery, an occupation Johnny Vojtaskovic found much more respectable than cooking. Right now Rob looked amused and slightly embarrassed at Shake's whites, as if his little brother had come to the table in a gorilla suit.

"Richard!" His mother's voice wasn't as loud as Johnny's, but it was more insistent. "Richard, babe!"

Outside his family, Shake hadn't answered to that name for a couple of decades. "Yeah, Momma?"

"You ain't gonna give us nothing too fancy to eat, are you? Because you know your father won't like it, and he gets the indigestion."

"No, Momma. I got a real nice meal planned for y'all. Nothing too fancy."

"I want to try the foie gras in chocolate sauce," Rob's wife, Suzy, piped up. Rob had e-mailed Shake to warn him that Suzy hung out on the local Internet dining boards and considered herself some kind of serious foodie, which struck nearly as much terror in Shake's heart as the presence of his blood relatives. He was proud of his foie gras *au chocolat,* though; he'd send it out for her and Rob while the old folks had his most popular app, the oysters and bacon with melted leeks on a crisp crouton. He'd been toying with the idea of renaming it Oysters La Pharmacie, making it his signature dish.

"Foie gras!" his father hollered. "What the hell is that?"

Rob smirked. "It's liver, Dad. You don't want any."

"I like a nice plate of liver and onions!"

"It's not calves' liver," Suzy said. "It's the liver of a duck force-fed to make it get great big and fat." She spoke deliberately and, Shake thought, a little sadistically—but he supposed being Johnny Vojtaskovic's daughter-in-law might well make one sadistic. She turned wide eyes on Shake. "Do you sear it or make a torchon?"

"Torchon," he said. Everybody who'd ever cooked at the Peychaud Grill knew how to make a perfect foie gras torchon. Paco Valdeon had drilled it into their heads that the connective tissue must be removed on an almost cellular level, and if a charcuterie plate ever came back with a microscopic shred of tissue on it, God help the cook who'd made the torchon that week.

"I think that's so much more original. *All* the chefs sear it these days."

It was true, but Shake couldn't help a small, inward eye-roll. Goddamn foodies were never content to just enjoy their meals; they always had to show you how *knowledgeable* they were.

"You can try the foie, Dad," he said. "I don't think you'll like it too much, though. I got some nice oysters for you and Momma."

"Plaquemines ersters, I hope!" The Vojtaskovic family had been working oyster beds in Plaquemines Parish since 1922. Upon his parents' retirement, Johnny had promptly sold his share of the beds, moved to the city, and bought the pest control business, but he still considered himself an oyster expert bar none.

"I wouldn't dare serve you any other kind. Look, I better go get started on your first courses. I'll check back with you in a little while."

Thank God they didn't read *Cornet*, he thought as he headed back to the kitchen. Suzy had probably seen his picture and the awful caption, but he hoped she was kind enough not to mention it to the others.

* * *

Suzy pulled the clipping out of her purse when they were halfway through the second course, a dark, rich squab and andouille gumbo. "Mr. V, Miz V, you saw this?"

"Aw, Suze, I told you not to show 'em that damn thing," said Rob, but his heart was not in the words.

Lydia Vojtaskovic took the little square of newsprint, squinted at it, and smiled, perceiving only that her son had appeared in print again. She had the *Big Easy* write-up framed and hanging in her kitchen. Suzy didn't like that much; even though Rob's work was much more important, managers from the Chalmette Refinery seldom got their pictures in *Big Easy*.

Lydia passed the clipping to Johnny, who brought it close to his eyes, then held it at arm's length, then scowled at it. "That's what they got him doing back there? Setting things on fire?"

He handed the clipping back to Lydia, who tried to return it to Suzy. "Oh, you can have it," Suzy said irritably. It hadn't had quite the damping effect she'd hoped; the elder Vojtaskovics addressed their sons by their Christian names and probably had no idea whether Richard's nickname was Shake or Snake, and the homosexual reference had gone over their heads entirely. She pursed her lips as the third course was set before them. "Oh, look, Robby," she said, "carpaccio."

"What the hell is that?" bellowed Johnny Vojtaskovic.

Dutifully, Shake never let two courses go by without checking on his family. He heard his father's opinion on the waiter ("He looks like a bum. What is he, Serbian?"), the décor ("I guess they got some Uptown fruit in here to do it"), the beautiful Jamaican bartender ("Who wants to look at some nappy-haired gal with an earring in her nose while they trying to drink their Scotch?"), and Shake's choice of shellfish in the ragout of clams and chorizo with garlic confit ("Well, they ain't ersters, that's for sure"). All of these *bon mots* were delivered at top volume, and by the time Orlando served dessert to the table—setting the plates down with a touch more force than was strictly necessary—Shake couldn't go anywhere in the restaurant without sensing mental laser beams of hostility aimed straight between his eyes.

He had thought they'd head home early. His parents had to drive all the way back to Slidell, where they'd moved a couple of years ago. Nevertheless, they remained at the table past closing time, adding wine and booze to his tab. "I'm going to start vacuuming around their feet," the hostess threatened the second time she came in the kitchen.

"Just let me finish breaking down. I'll get rid of 'em."

He hurried through his closing tasks, then went out to the dining room. Suzy was drinking a twenty-seven-dollar glass of ice wine. Everybody else had Scotch—not the well brand, Shake was betting. Johnny produced a cigarillo and would have lit it off the candle had Lydia not deftly plucked it from his fingers. "Gimme that!" shouted Johnny, stricken.

"There's no smoking in these fancy restaurants, Mr. V," Suzy said viciously. "It's not good for the *palate.*" She flashed Shake a commiserating yet somehow superior little smile.

In the end, Shake had to sit with them for fifteen minutes and drop several increasingly broad hints before he finally got them to finish up their drinks and start moving toward the door. "I really hope y'all liked it," he said as he waited with them for the valet.

"It wasn't too bad," Johnny admitted. "But next time, let us relax a little after dinner—you don't gotta rush us out!"

Shake watched them drive away, hoping half-heartedly that they wouldn't plunge off the Twin Spans. He wouldn't mind so much if Rob and Suzy hit an open drawbridge on their way back to Arabi, but he'd never heard of that happening except in the movies. When both cars were out of sight, he went back into the restaurant, lowered his aching carcass onto a barstool, and dropped his head into his hands. Before he could order a drink, Orlando swooped down upon him to report further disgraces: "They didn't leave a *tip.*"

Shake dug out his wallet and handed over two twenties. He'd been planning to grab lunch up the street at Casamento's the next day, but there went his fried oyster loaf and dozen on the half shell; he guessed he'd be eating cereal instead.

Orlando looked at Shake as if he'd have preferred arguing to getting the money, but Shake stared him down, and finally the waiter took himself off to do whatever career waiters did when they got off work—get drunk and practice insulting each other, maybe. "Can I please have some of that Scotch my folks were drinking?" Shake asked the bartender.

"Get it yourself," she told him. "This *nappy-haired gal's* going home."

XIV

THE GADWALL HAS LANDED

In the early 1930s, the Levee Board built a V-shaped seawall in Lake Pontchartrain and filled the V with six million cubic yards of mud from the lake bottom. These were (and remain) the sort of labors required to create land above sea level in New Orleans. Once they had the land, they built a state-of-the-art airport on it. Huey Long caused the airport to be named for Levee Board president Abraham Shushan, a longtime cog in his political machine. Its grand opening the weekend before Mardi Gras 1934 was heralded by a crashing thunderstorm that drove sodden dignitaries into the hangars. Not too long after that, Long was assassinated and Shushan was accused (though never convicted) of laundering money for his campaign. The new governor—a reform man, in name anyway—insisted that thirty-two hundred imprints of Shushan's name be removed from the airport. Glass was scraped clean, ashtrays painted, door handles filed down. The place was unimaginatively renamed the New Orleans Lakefront Airport.

Rickey learned some of this from posters in the terminal lobby. He also learned that Mr. Shushan had eventually died in a plane crash, which seemed a gratuitously cruel twist of fate. Though he hadn't known the history of the airport and had never had occasion to fly out of it—Lakefront mostly handled private and charter flights these days—Rickey had been coming here since he was almost a baby. He remembered sitting on the observation deck with his parents, watching the planes land and take off. They couldn't have come as close to the terminal as he remembered, but the noise had been thrilling and a little scary. On one wondrous occasion, the Goodyear Blimp was tethered in the field between runways, its elephantine bulk trembling in the lake breeze. Or so he recalled; probably it had been tied down too tightly to move at all.

He'd gotten here early today because he wanted a look at the place, and was gratified to see that aside from the disappearance of the observation deck—a casualty of Homeland Security, he guessed—Lakefront Airport hadn't changed a bit since he'd last seen it twenty-odd years ago. The terminal was still an art deco fantasy of glossy colored marble and brass. The little restaurant still served reconstituted Sysco soups and odd sandwiches. You could still fold yourself into an old-fashioned phone booth and make a call, though it cost fifty cents now. Rickey had two quarters in his pocket, so he parked his butt on the deeply scratched but highly polished little wooden ledge and called home. "Hey, man."

"Hey, man." It was their day off, and Rickey could hear a TiVo'd basketball game in the background. "Ducks on the ground yet?"

"No, but the flight's on time. Listen, you want to meet me over at the restaurant after I get 'em?"

"What for?"

"I thought maybe we ought to break one down, cook a breast and a leg in some real simple way. You know, get a feel for the meat. I never had wild duck before, did you?"

"I don't think so, but it can't be all that different, huh?"

"G, you know what happens when you *assume?* You make an *ass—"*

"I know, I know. But why don't you just bring one home? I don't want to spend our day off at the restaurant."

"Well, I kinda thought we might go ahead and start on some stuff. You know, like the confit and the prosciutto."

The sound G-man made was not precisely a whimper, but Rickey wasn't sure what else to call it.

"You just want to lay around and watch hoops, huh?"

"Well..."

"C'mon, G, the season's hardly even started yet."

"Yeah, but that's the best time, because anything's still possible."

"Uh huh, and when it's midseason you'll say *that's* the best time because it's just starting to get exciting, and when they playoffs start you'll say *that's the best time because dude, it's the playoffs."*

G-man laughed at the accurate imitation of his voice, then grew serious. "I know, dude, but I got that bone in my foot again. It was killing me all last night. I really wanted to rest today."

"OK, OK," Rickey said, knowing when he was beaten. G-man wasn't a complainer. If he said he wanted to rest, he probably needed to. Rickey would do him the favor of pretending Steve Nash and Amare Stoudemire were just added bonuses.

They hung up, and within five minutes, the plane Rickey was waiting for taxied down the runway. Tee Fontenot had told him, "Look for the guy with no tie," and sure enough, everybody who disembarked had a tie on except for one barrel-shaped, silver-haired man.

"Mr. Schexnaydre?" Rickey was pretty sure he'd mangled the name. Apparently it was a common one in Cajun country, but he'd never heard it until his phone conversation with Fontenot a couple of days ago.

"Chef!" The guy seized his hand, gave it three hard pumps. "Got your ducks, yeah! They're coming off the plane in a minute—let's see if we can't get somebody to help us load 'em in your car."

"I got it."

"You sure? It's twelve big coolers, pretty heavy."

"We can make several trips." In truth, Rickey wouldn't have minded help, but he pictured Schexnaydre snapping his fingers at some random black person—*Say, boy!* He knew the rest of Louisiana wasn't the unmitigated hotbed of race-baiting fundamentalism some New Orleanians tried to pretend it was, but old suspicions died hard.

In the end, Rickey borrowed a dolly from the baggage handlers and dealt with most of the load himself while Schexnaydre tagged along behind talking about the golf courses, fishing areas, and hunting grounds he planned to visit on this trip, none of which was actually in New Orleans. The ducks were packed in Styrofoam coolers with the names of species scrawled on the outsides: TEAL, GADWALL, DOS GRIS. "Tee said to let you know you'll get some of the late arrivals at the banquet," Schexnaydre said.

"Diners?"

"Ducks. These are the ones that come through early in the season."

"OK."

"You don't hunt?"

Rickey thought of the one time he'd fired a real gun: a friend's uncle's nine-millimeter. The friend, a Lower Ninth Ward kid who'd since been in and out of Orleans Parish Prison and would probably graduate to Angola eventually, had swiped the gun from a drawer and carried it to a vacant lot near the river for the other kids to gawk at. They'd taken turns firing at a telephone pole, scattering like droplets of water in a hot skillet at the first sound of police sirens. He'd rather enjoyed the feel of all that firepower in his hand, but with the possible exception of a few bosses he'd had, he couldn't see himself firing it at anything alive. "Nope," he said. "Don't get out of the city much."

Schexnaydre made a face. "Never heard of that stopping some of these...people. You can have New Orleans. Don't know how you stand it."

"I like it," Rickey said in a tone of voice that actually shut the man up for a couple of minutes.

They were wedging the last cooler into the backseat of Rickey's Plymouth when Schexnaydre said, "I'm the one who recommended you to Ducks Unlimited, you know."

Rickey looked up at him. "Thought you said you hated New Orleans."

"What can I say? I'm not a city boy. Appreciate a good meal, though. I've eaten at your restaurant three or four times now. Think you got most of the famous places beat all to hell."

The famous *places?* Rickey decided he was about ready for this guy to get on with his golfing, fishing, and hunting. "Well, thanks for the good word."

"Sure thing." Schexnaydre winked. "You gonna take care of me next time I come in, huh?"

"You know it."

And Rickey would. Schexnaydre might be a bit of an asshole, but if he was telling the truth, he'd done them a favor. In the restaurant business, you took care of people you knew, people who'd done you favors, people who claimed to have done you favors. Even if you didn't particularly like them, you made sure they had a good waiter, sent out an extra course, comped their drinks or desserts. If you didn't, you could be sure everybody they knew would hear about it. It was just the way things worked.

Nonetheless, he was happy to take his leave of the great white hunter and head back into town, his car laden with ducks. He couldn't wait to see how they handled. Rickey was a little too old to like work above all else, but he still felt an unparalleled excitement when he got his hands on something he'd never cooked before.

At the restaurant, he unloaded the twelve coolers and stashed them in the walk-in. Though his back had begun to ache, he felt the strong rush of well-being he always experienced when he was alone in the restaurant. No other cooks to fuck things up, no waiters to nag him, no customers to bitch and moan and expect special treatment. Of course he needed the cooks and waiters and customers, but once in a while it was nice to have the place all to himself. He sat in the dining room for a few minutes, not trying to imagine it from a customer's perspective, not thinking about the kitchen or wanting a drink, just enjoying the good place he had created.

His research suggested that teal was a good training duck, so after a little while he walked back through the kitchen, opened the cooler marked BW TEAL, and selected a plastic-wrapped package that felt heavier than it looked. He hummed "Born Free" under his breath as he carried it out to the car.

As he entered the house, G-man hollered "Duck!" and threw a Nerf basketball at him. Rickey bobbled the ball, then caught it in the hand that wasn't holding the bagged bird.

"What? You been sitting here planning that the whole time I was gone?"

"Pretty much. Game's a total blowout."

"Well, c'mon in the kitchen and help me see about this bird."

G-man got up and limped after him.

"Your foot still fucked up?"

"Aw, it's not too bad. How's your back?"

Rickey shrugged.

"Couple old geezers," G-man said ruefully.

"I know it, Gramps. You feel like taking a whack at the butchering? You always been better at cutting things up."

"Sure, hand me that Wüsthof..." G-man set the knife on the countertop, reached into the bag Rickey had brought home. "Aagh!"

"What? Jeez, dude, what is it?"

"Feathers!"

"You're fucking kidding me."

G-man pulled the duck out of the bag and brandished it at Rickey, his hand wrapped around its neck. From the top of his fist emerged a tiny, slit-eyed, unmistakably duck-billed head. From the bottom hung a brown, blue, and white body that had been gutted, but not deprived of its feathers or its webby feet. The ooze from a small perforation stained its delicately dappled breast.

"Jesus Christ."

"Least we know it's fresh."

"Goddammit, you mean we gotta pull the feathers off fifty ducks?"

"*We* don't." G-man gazed at Rickey over the tops of his shades. "Jacolvy and Devonte do. Or the dishwashers, even."

"Whatever. We still lose two pair of hands. And I don't want the dishwashers doing it—they might tear the skin." Rickey stewed for a minute, then got over it; the ducks had come the way they had come and there was no point in agonizing. "Give it here. I'll pull the goddamn feathers out."

"You want me to cut off the head and feet first?"

"No...oh, shit, G, I don't know. This is fucking gross."

"No it's not. It's the same thing you cook with every day—this is just what it really looks like. Probably good for us to deal with real animals once in a while instead of getting all our meat in cute little packages."

"I cut down a pork leg just last week. I don't think a whole pork leg is a *cute little package.*"

"Maybe not, but it sure ain't a pig." G-man took a cleaver out of the drawer, slapped the teal on the cutting board, and lopped off its head with one neat stroke. Two more strokes and the legs fell into the sink. Although he knew G-man was right, Rickey still felt a little nauseous; he was pretty sure nobody had ever been decapitated in his kitchen before.

They sat at the table with the sad little body between them, pinching feathers and yanking them out. It was hard at first, but grew easier once they got the hang of it. Rickey was no longer particularly grossed out, but he felt a little sad at first. They used premium meats at the restaurant—Niman Ranch pork, free-range chickens, no hormone-pumped beef—but he didn't kid himself into thinking most of the animals whose flesh he cooked had led wonderful lives. If you were a farm animal, even on a high-end farm, you were pretty much screwed from the moment of birth (or hatching). This bird, though, had lived free in the Louisiana marsh, some of the most fragile and beautiful land in the world. Rickey hadn't spent much time out there, but even driving one of the narrow roads through the wetlands would imprint them on your heart forever. He pictured the duck and its mate flying over the marsh at dusk, moss-fraught cypress trees and grass hummocks black against the sky, water reflecting the smeary oranges, pinks, and grays of the sunset. The birds coasted in and landed, seeming to run across the surface of the water as their wings scooped the air, iridescent baffles.

Then he shrugged. At least they'd had some pleasure in their lives. Unless you were going to become a vegetarian, which he sure as hell wasn't, he guessed you ought to be able to think about stuff like this and deal with the meat anyway. G-man was right as usual.

When they had all but the pinfeathers off, Rickey singed the skin with his crème brûlée torch, burning away the fuzz and stubble that remained. A smell somewhere between burning hair and melting plastic filled the kitchen. Rickey consulted his notes as G-man cut the bird into pieces and put the carcass in a big pot to cook down for stock. From his cookbooks and some game websites, he'd gathered that wild ducks varied dramatically in their fat content depending on the breed, the season, and where they'd been shot. They started out plump up north, but by the time they got all the way down to Louisiana, they could be pretty lean.

G-man handed him a breast. Rickey palpated it thoughtfully, cooking it ten different ways in his mind before he applied any actual heat. It was smaller, denser, and way darker than a domestic duck breast, and didn't seem to have much of a fat layer between the skin and the muscle. The kind of meat that would overcook in a heartbeat. Rickey decided he'd brine both breasts, wrap this one in bacon and leave the other one plain, sauté them both, compare the results. Normally you'd brine a whole bird, but since this one was already cut up, he'd leave the breasts in saltwater for only ninety minutes or so—long enough to keep them juicy (he hoped) without too much salt getting into the meat. In the meantime, he'd experiment with the legs.

Thirty minutes later they sat down to their first taste of wild duck: a single small thigh sautéed in olive oil with turnips, onions, and whole cloves of garlic. Rickey had cooked it just until the skin was crisp, but he had been able to feel the muscle fibers shrinking when he prodded the meat in the pan, ands sure enough, the first bite was tough and dry.

"Don't worry about it," G-man said when he saw Rickey's discouraged expression. "You said yourself we're mostly gonna be doing confit with the legs. That won't be dry. Taste these vegetables—the flavor's great."

Rickey forked up a turnip cube and chewed it slowly. There hadn't been much fat to flavor them, but they were still permeated with a dark, rich essence, salty and complex, a little bloody. Rickey supposed this was the taste people called "gamy" and wrinkled their noses at. Well, the Ducks Unlimited people wouldn't be wrinkling their noses. Neither would Bobby Hebert, who in true Cajun fashion talked on the radio about eating snapping turtle *(cowan)* and oyster drills *(bigarneau)* during his youth in South Lafourche Parish. A little gaminess wouldn't faze them; Rickey just had to cook the goddamn shit right. The thought heartened him. He didn't quite know how to do it yet, but he'd figure it out.

They cooked the breasts mid-rare and sauced them very simply with a mushroom demiglace G-man found in the freezer. The plain breast was even drier and tougher than the thigh had been, but the bacon-wrapped one was exquisitely moist. "We're getting there," said G-man, tucking a thick slice into his mouth.

"One down, forty-nine to go."

XVI

BIG NIGHT

Amuse of Gadwall en Daube Glacé

Gumbo of Pintail and Poche's Andouille Sausage

Confit of Dos Gris with Arugula, Radicchio, Cracklins, and Satsuma-Bacon Vinaigrette

Butter-Poached Drum Wrapped in Wood Duck Prosciutto with Porcini-Garlic Jam

Braised Teal with Dried Cherries and Kirsch

Savory Bread Pudding with Greenhead, Chestnuts, and Green Apples

Palate Cleanser of Juniper Sorbet

Crème Brûlée Flavored With Dos Gris Fat, Served with a Triangle of Crispy Duck Skin

Rickey seldom felt constrained by the liquor gimmick, but he was glad to get a break from it. Still, he hadn't been able to resist adding a little kirsch to the Elizabeth David recipe. His restaurant deserved a nod, at least.

"Pretty jiggy fish dish," G-man said when Rickey showed him the rough menu.

"I think it'll be real good."

"Hey, jiggy's a compliment. I like the juniper sorbet, too. Carries out the game theme."

"That's what I thought," Rickey said modestly.

There had been a certain amount of angst regarding the dessert course. Tanker wanted to do a caramel wonton filled with shredded duck confit. He'd served a similar wonton at Liquor with a foie gras mousse filling and it had been spectacularly good, but the dish just wasn't plausible for three hundred. "I can't have you fucking around with hot caramel half the evening," Rickey said. "We need you on the line. The dessert's gotta be pretty simple, something you can prep up in advance."

As well, Rickey also wasn't crazy about the idea of trotting the duck confit back out for an encore performance, but he didn't tell Tanker that; he knew Tanker would just suggest that he do something else for his salad course.

"Simple!" Tanker groused. "*You* get to do all the fancy shit in the world, but desserts gotta be simple. Desserts get no respect."

"You'll thank me when you're slamming out crème brûlées instead of folding up three hundred fiddly little wontons," Rickey said. "I saw you making those things, remember? You were cussing balls-out and burning your fingers, and you only had to do about fifty."

Against G-man's wishes, Rickey had gone ahead with his plan to close Liquor the weekend of the banquet. He wasn't crazy about it himself, but there was just no way to stretch the crew thinly enough to cover the restaurant and the Ducks Unlimited dinner without sacrificing quality at one place, probably both. Of all the things that made Rickey crazy, the idea of willingly sacrificing an iota of quality gnawed at him the most ferociously. Closing would cut into their profits a little, but not as much as regular customers getting bad meals ultimately would. People never forgot that shit, they never forgave you for it, and most times they never came back—just told all their friends and Internet cronies how you'd fallen off.

It wasn't just the potential loss of revenue that gnawed at him, though; he simply couldn't stomach the idea of serving a dish that was less than the best he and his crew could make. He supposed that was one of the things that had kept him in business this long even though he'd never headed a kitchen before opening his own restaurant. It also made him a royal pain in the ass to work for, he knew, but that couldn't be helped.

So the crew was going to caravan to Opelousas in three vehicles: Rickey, G-man, and most of the food in one car; Tanker, Terrance, Marquis, and the rest of the food in a second; Devonte, Jacolvy, and the two dishwashers in a third. They planned to get there the afternoon before the banquet, spend part of that night and all the next day setting up. Everybody would stay over two nights in the motel rooms Tee Fontenot had booked for them. The day after the banquet, the younger cooks and dishwashers would drive back to New Orleans. Rickey and G-man would stay over an extra night to check out the town and maybe eat some boudin. Tanker and Terrance could do whatever they liked.

That was the basic plan. Rickey wasn't naïve enough to think it would go exactly as he'd laid it out, but he hoped for no major deviations.

The drive was an easy three hours on the I-10. G-man took the first turn driving. Actually, Rickey would be happy if G-man decided to take *all* the turns driving; it wasn't one of his favorite things. They had soaped the legend **D*U*C*K** on the rear windshields of all three cars, as if they were a caravan of culinary surgeons hurrying to administer good taste to some war-torn region. **D*U*C*K** didn't actually stand for anything, but Rickey figured nobody would give a shit.

Past Baton Rouge, the interstate turned into a long bridge over the Atchafalaya Basin. Living and dead cypress trunks rose from an eternity of duckweed, swamp water, pale reflected sky. A faint clean aroma of duck fat emanated from the sealed containers in the backseat. They'd both been quiet for about fifteen miles, each lost in his own thoughts, when G-man said, "It's a really great menu."

"I know." It was a conceited thing to say, but Rickey *did* think it was a great menu, and G-man didn't expect false modesty from him. "I didn't even spend all that much time on it. When I went to write it down, it was like it just came to me."

"Cause you'd been thinking about it since September. It was forming in...you know...your subconscious mind."

"I guess."

"See, that's why you're a genius."

Rickey's first response to the word genius was not pleasure, but a mixture of embarrassment and alarm. "I'm not—" He realized it was meant as a compliment. "Well, goddamn, I don't know about all that. I got a little talent. It might've helped me design the menu, but it's not gonna get me through tomorrow night."

"That's why we got a good crew."

"Yeah," Rickey said. He stared out the window. That *genius* still nagged at him. What had made G-man say such a thing? Once, when he was still reading the online dining forums, he'd seen himself described as a "culinary savant." When he looked up *savant* in the dictionary, the first definition was *A person of profound or extensive learning;* the second was *One who performs by rote or instinct rather than great intelligence; idiot savant.* He'd decided he didn't want to know which definition the person on the message board had meant.

He hung on for twenty more miles, almost to their turnoff onto I-49, before he could stand it no longer. "What the hell did you have to say that for?"

"Say what?"

"What you said I was."

"A genius?" G-man glanced over at Rickey, who was slumped against the passenger door. "I don't know. It's what I think. I meant it in a nice way."

"I just don't like you setting me apart like that. It makes me feel weird. I'm not some kinda egghead. I'm the same as you."

"Rickey, if you were the same as me, we'd still be on the line in somebody else's restaurant. Don't give me that bullshit. There's nothing wrong with being a genius—you're probably the only person in the world who thinks it's an insult. Now quit leaning against that door before you fly out."

This last was something G-man's mother had often said to them when they rode in her car as kids, and Rickey was surprised into a laugh. He couldn't quite leave the matter alone, though: "Well, I don't like it."

G-man lifted his hands a couple of inches off the steering wheel. "I'm sorry. I'm sorry. I promise I'll never do it again."

Five more miles of quiet. They passed a big yellow billboard advertising a Cajun meat market. A grinning pig in a chef's hat offered steaming boudin links, boudin balls, andouille, cracklins. All the savory products of the boucherie, the Acadian tradition that turned every part of the pig into something irresistible. Rickey realized he hadn't eaten since early the evening before. He'd just begun to wonder why he wasn't hungry, even in the face of such temptation, when G-man said, "You nervous about meeting Bobby?"

"Seems like if I was, you wouldn't want to get me started thinking about it."

"I rather you think about it now, talk about it now, get it over with. You're not gonna have time to be nervous tomorrow."

"Well, that's just it. I'm a little nervous now, but tomorrow night I'll be in the zone. Bobby's gonna be just another mouth to me." He saw G-man's look. "Well, an *important* mouth. But he's a team leader, you know? He's not gonna be impressed unless he sees us get *everybody's* meal right."

"I guess you got a point there."

"Course I do. Anyway, aren't *you* nervous?"

G-man shrugged. "I was always more of a Rickey Jackson man."

"Figures," Rickey said. "Protect the quarterback. Dome Patrol. Hell, G, you're my Kitchen Patrol."

"I never had the bulk to be a linebacker."

"Yeah, but if kitchen chops were muscle, you'd have the bulk of four guys."

"Aw, jeez." G-man shook his head as he made the turn onto 49. "Now you're just getting back at me for calling you a genius."

* * *

The Delta Grand wasn't what Rickey had expected. From Tee Fontenot's description of a "historic theatre," he'd envisioned something posh and elegant, maybe in an art deco style. Instead their venue was an average-looking building in the heart of Opelousas' small, old-fashioned downtown, across the street from the courthouse square and right next to the jail. The lobby was decorated with posters for teen dances and hip-hop shows. Fontenot had said he and a bunch of the banquet organizers would be hunting today, and no one was there to greet Rickey and G-man when they arrived, but the door was unlocked and they started carrying stuff inside.

The kitchen was no French Laundry, but it would do: a large, high-ceilinged industrial space with a long hot line, four big stovetops, and a half-dozen rolling steam tables that Rickey planned to push out of the way. Tanker, Terrance, and Marquis arrived about twenty minutes later in Terrance's

Oldsmobile, carrying the rest of the food. They went to work putting things away, rearranging, scoping things out. Rickey found the rest of his ducks in one of the tall reach-in coolers, but he couldn't put Devonte and Jacolvy to work plucking feathers, because they weren't here yet.

He pulled out his cell phone and called Devonte. The younger man answered after six rings. In the background, Rickey could hear a thumping bass—not Devonte's considerable car stereo, because there was also muffled laughter and the sound of an announcer saying, "Give it up for TAMIKA!"

"Where the hell are you?"

"Oh! Uh...Chef?"

Rickey closed his eyes, breathed deeply, and reminded himself that wherever Devonte and Jacolvy were, they had his only dishwashers with them. "Yeah, D," he said. "This is Chef. Standing here in the kitchen of the goddamn banquet hall"—his voice started to rise, but he got control of it—"just wondering where my pantry guys are."

"Uh, well, we just stopped off for a drink. Got thirsty drivin. We on our way right now."

"That's right," Rickey heard Jacolvy say, or maybe it was one of the dishwashers.

"Fine, but where *are* you? As in geographically?"

"Where we at?" Devonte asked somebody on his end. There was a lot of whispering, then: "Say someplace called Bayou Goula."

"Bayou *Goula?*" That was not only way the hell south of the interstate, but on the opposite side of the river from where they should have been. "How the fuck did you get there?"

"We got off in Baton Rouge lookin for a place to get a drink. Got lost."

"And found yourselves at the nearest strip club, huh?" Devonte started to speak, but Rickey cut him off. "Forget it. I don't want to hear about it right now. What I *want* is for you to still have a *job* tomorrow, and for Jacolvy not to violate his *parole* by being *underage* in a fucking *titty bar.* And in order to make that *happen,* D, you need to stand up right now, wipe that stupid fucking smirk off your face, get the rest of my crew out of there, get directions back to the interstate, and drive due west until you hit Lafayette. At that point you need to turn north onto I-49 and proceed directly to Opelousas. Don't stop for another drink. Don't stop to pee. Don't stop to wipe your *dick* on some hoochie momma's *G-string.* You understand what I'm telling you?"

"Yeah, Chef. Sorry."

"And if you got that kid drunk, you can goddamn well dump him off at the motel and pluck all these goddamn birds yourself."

"Awright, Chef."

"You *heard* me?"

"Yeah, Chef."

Rickey snapped his phone shut, more mad at himself for allowing that bunch to ride together than anything else. Jacolvy was nineteen, Devonte twenty-two, the dishwashers not much older. None of them had ever been out of New Orleans before; it was hardly surprising that they'd be tempted to go off looking for trouble. He should have made Marquis ride with them—no, Terrance. Marquis might have gone right along to the titty bar, but Terrance wouldn't have put up with it. Rickey wondered what other missteps he'd made in his planning, what other errors lurked ahead like rakes in tall grass just waiting for him to step on them.

The youngsters arrived a couple of hours later, shamefaced, ready to work, smelling only a little of beer and scarcely at all of weed. It wasn't long before they were sitting on opposite sides of a big plastic trashcan, exclaiming with disgust as they plunged their fingers into refrigerator-chilled feathers.

* * *

They were busy setting up and prepping until almost midnight. Probably some of the stuff could have waited until tomorrow, but as Rickey announced to the crew, "We need to get our ducks in a row." It wasn't until they started groaning and booing him that he realized what he'd said.

He and G-man wanted a drink. They strolled through the square and along the streets, certain they'd find something open—this was still south Louisiana, after all—but the downtown was deserted. The central block seemed to have been bombed out entirely. Most of it had been occupied by a big department store that still bore traces of bygone elegance—gold lettering that said ABDALLA'S on the doors, colored tile mosaics in the entryways—but standing on those mosaics and peering through those doors, they could see burned beams, holes in the ceiling with moonlight streaming through, black mold and eerily verdant ferns swarming up the walls. Merchandise still lay scattered here and there, men's ties and ladies' blouses thirty years out of date, an easy chair rotting in a display window.

The rest of the downtown was similar: an old Rexall drugstore with blinded windows, a defunct dollar-and-dime store, something called the Archway Lounge that gave them hope at first, but turned out to be just a scorched and gutted brick space full of weeds, trash, and empty pints of liquors they'd never heard of. Crystal Palace gin, Barking Colonel bourbon. There were still scattered businesses trying to make a go of it, and obviously there was some money in the town, but something had struck a blow to the heart of it. G-man shivered. "Let's just get in the car," he said. "Maybe we'll find something if we drive."

They drove around the entire town twice and couldn't find anywhere that seemed to be open except a couple of ramshackle lounges with pickup trucks and motorcycles parked outside. "I don't feel like dealing with some big zydeco scene,"

Rickey said. "Everybody in there's gonna be dancing, playing washboards, wrestling alligators with their bare hands."

"Yeah, and there's always a Mardi Gras parade going on in New Orleans and we all drink Hurricanes on Bourbon Street all the time."

"What?"

"Stereotypes."

Rickey shrugged. "I just don't feel like socializing. We'll have to do enough of that tomorrow night."

They drove on to the motel, a low structure built in an L shape around a patch of asphalt. A pall of roasting pork aroma hung over the downtown area. "They must leave it to slow-cook all night, then make boudin in the morning," Rickey said.

"Wish I had some boudin right now."

"Day after tomorrow. We get this dinner done, then we get to be tourists."

In the motel office, a bedraggled parrot in a cage eyed them, then said quietly, "Bugger." They were forced to endure its scrutiny for ten minutes before they could raise anyone to check them in. Rickey dug out a pint of Wild Turkey he kept in the car for emergencies and sat on the edge of the hard mattress sipping straight from the bottle. The room was marginally clean and aggressively threadbare. The only amenity was a piece of soap the size of a postage stamp in the shower stall, which was visible from the bed. Somebody cursed audibly on the other side of the wall, then fell silent. All things considered, Rickey felt more comfortable here than in the gilded Dallas hotel he'd once been booked into.

G-man stretched out on the bed and flexed his foot, trying to pop the bones in his toes. After another two swigs of Wild Turkey, Rickey scooted back on the bed, lifted G-man's sore foot onto his lap, and started rubbing the sole. It was really the top of his foot that gave G-man misery, but Rickey's thumbs felt so good on his instep that he decided not to say anything.

"I don't know if I'm ready for this," Rickey said.

"You can quit if it stinks."

Rickey pinched G-man's big toe. "No, asshole, I mean the dinner. I'm freaking out a little."

"How come? We're in good shape with the prep and we got a great menu. What's to freak out about?"

"I don't know." Abruptly, Rickey pushed G-man's foot away, stood, and went to the door. He opened it and stood looking out over the parking lot. The night was clear and warm for December. After a couple of minutes, a greasy-looking little man came wandering along the breezeway, saw Rickey standing there, and said, "Hey, bro, where you from? Got a dollar?"

The guy stood looking expectantly up at Rickey, who didn't appear to have heard him. Gradually the panhandler's expression changed from lazy anticipation to confusion to alarm, and he hurried away. Rickey shut the door and stood in the middle of the room staring around as if he'd forgotten where he was. He had a wild look in his eye that G-man didn't like at all. It was easy to see why the greasy-looking guy had gotten nervous.

"I just got a bad feeling. We forgot something, or something's gonna happen out of our control. Something's gonna go wrong."

"Rickey!" G-man said sharply.

"We never should've agreed to do this, what the fuck do we know about doing banquets, we're just gonna embarrass ourselves in front of Bobby Hebert and everybody, Ducks Unlimited is gonna ask for their money back—"

G-man sighed, heaved himself up off the bed. His foot felt a little better from resting and being rubbed, and he managed to make it across the room without limping, though of course "across the room" only entailed about three steps. He gripped Rickey's shoulders and gave him a little shake. "Rickey!"

"*What?*"

"Quit it! What are you, some whining little pantry bitch? Get ahold of yourself!"

"But G—"

"But nothing. We're not having that. Now, come here. Lay down." G-man didn't particularly enjoy talking to the love of his life the way he'd address a trained dog, but that was just the way it had to be sometimes. There was no real rhyme or reason to it. The night before they opened the restaurant, Rickey had been as cool as a spearmint snowball, but he'd had a total meltdown about two weeks later: bawling his head off, saying he didn't know what he was doing, wanting to go sit on a beach somewhere, the whole nine yards. Once that was over with, he'd gotten on with the business of running the restaurant. You never knew with Rickey. Just when you expected him to get hysterical, he'd likely as not stare down the situation and do what needed to be done. Other times, the least little mishap could send him down the pike.

G-man wasn't letting him go down the pike this time, though. There was too much at stake, not just for the restaurant but for Rickey personally. If he worked himself into a frenzy tonight and his work tomorrow suffered as a result, he'd never forgive himself. G-man pushed him gently onto the bed and lay down beside him, one hand on his chest, the other stroking the back of his neck. Gradually, Rickey's fists unclenched and his breathing slowed.

"You gonna be OK?"

"Yeah, I think so."

"You ready for this dinner?"

"Yeah."

"What are we gonna do if something goes wrong?"

"We're gonna handle it."

"There you go."

Rickey leaned over to the nightstand, got the Wild Turkey and swigged again, lay back down.

"If I make you come, do you think you could go to sleep?" G-man said.

"I don't want to fuck in this room. The bed's too hard and the walls are too thin."

"We don't have to fuck. We can just mess around."

"I don't know. I think I got too much on my mind."

G-man waited. Just to amuse himself, he started counting in his head. He'd gotten halfway to a hundred when Rickey said, "Mess around how?"

By morning, the weather had turned gray and leaden. It still wasn't cold, but it was getting there. This change made Rickey happy: he had designed a seasonal menu and people would enjoy his food more if it felt something like winter outside. The pall of pork was gone. They woke up the rest of the crew, found coffee, headed en masse to the Delta Grand, and began the day-long prep regimen that would take them right up to the banquet at seven this evening. Rickey was glad they still had a lot to do. He didn't want any downtime to think about possible mishaps. He was stirring the roux for the gumbo, waiting for the vast batch of oil and flour to turn from light golden-brown to the nut-brown that would give it a dark, rich flavor, when Schexnaydre walked into the kitchen with another man. "Chef! Good to see you again. I'd like to introduce our president, Tee Fontenot."

Rickey turned away from the stove. When he saw Fontenot, his jaw dropped, and he immediately felt bad; an instant later he realized it couldn't matter. There were no dark glasses, no white cane, but it was immediately evident from the milkiness of his eyes and the tilt of his head that Fontenot was blind.

He either didn't notice that Rickey had missed a beat or was polite enough to ignore it. His grip on Rickey's hand was surprisingly strong, but why should that be surprising? Losing your sight didn't mean your muscles atrophied. "Good to finally meet you," he said in that musical Cajun accent. "Sure does smell fine in here. Those ducks cooking up nice?"

"Real nice. Took me a little while to figure things out, but now I really like cooking with them. They're beautiful."

"They better be. I shot some of 'em myself."

A smile creased Fontenot's leathery face, and Rickey had time to wonder if he was being fucked with. Then Schexnaydre said, "Tee, we better get out of here and let these boys do their thing."

"Yeah, otherwise we won't get nothing to eat tonight. Ain't that right, Chef?"

"Yessir."

Fontenot cackled as if Rickey had made a witticism and turned away. Schexnaydre's fingers barely touched his elbow, guiding but not leading him; he seemed to navigate pretty well. Surely he couldn't really shoot ducks on the wing, though?

"Bobby Hebert in town yet?" Rickey called after them.

Fontenot half-turned toward the sound of his voice. "Nope! Duck hunting down in Lafourche! He's coming in this afternoon—on a helicopter!"

"You flying the helicopter, too?" said G-man. Rickey stared at him, and G-man looked horrified at himself, as if the words had popped out of his mouth before he could stop them. Even Schexnaydre was taken aback, but Fontenot slapped his leg and whooped.

"Flying the helicopter, me! That's a good one! You heard that, Schex? Flying the helicopter! I oughta ride along and get the pilot to let me take the controls for a minute! See old Bobby's face! Oh, Lord!"

The volume of these comments dwindled as Schexnaydre led Fontenot out of the kitchen, but they could hear him going right up until he climbed into Schexnaydre's quad cab in the rear parking lot.

"You think he really shot some of these ducks?" Terrance said.

"Who knows." Rickey shook his head. "We're in another world, man."

"You got that right."

Rickey unpacked his hotel pans of confit. He scraped away the top layer of melted fat that had covered the meat for two weeks, sealing in its juices and permeating it with flavor. He didn't keep confit on the menu all the time, but customers raved about it when he ran it as a special, said it was the best in town. His big secret was replacing a quarter of the duck fat with pork lard, which deepened the taste without overwhelming the duck. Most people couldn't identify the magic ingredient; they just knew it was bone-gnawingly good confit. This time he'd had to augment the wild duck fat with store-bought, and nobody would be gnawing the bones since he was shredding the meat off of them to serve in little haystacks on the salad. Still a decent batch, though, he confirmed by popping a dark, oily chunk of thigh into his mouth. Thoroughly laced with fat, it all but melted on his tongue.

By four o'clock, everything was as prepped as it could be for the moment. Glistening mounds of daube glacé nestled in endive leaves in the fridge, perfect little bites waiting to amuse hungry mouths. Salad greens chilled on plates, ready for a dollop of confit and a ladle of satsuma-bacon vinaigrette. Pots of gumbo warmed gently in water baths. Bread puddings were assembled, waiting to go into ovens. In the freezer, three hundred perfect balls of juniper sorbet sat in three hundred Chinese soup spoons. Rickey had thought the white sorbet would look nice in the white spoons. When he prepared a sample dish, though, he didn't like the monochrome effect. He'd been momentarily frustrated: using artificial colors seemed pointless and dishonest, but anything natural—beet juice, saffron—would alter the juniper flavor. Tanker had saved the day by showing him how to make liquid chlorophyll out of pureed spinach strained through several thicknesses of cheesecloth. It had a clean, slightly grassy taste that went well with the juniper, and the mint-green balls looked really good in the spoons. Like something from the cover of a glossy food magazine, Rickey thought, though not even torture could have made him say it out loud.

Banquet service differed radically from the way they usually ran their kitchen. Instead of cooks working different stations, all seven of them would work on each course in a kind of assembly-line procedure: two three-man teams plus one guy running around making sure everything was going smoothly. To prepare the braised teal, for instance, G-man would warm up the already-cooked duck breasts in the ovens and get the warmed plates from the dishwashers. Meanwhile, Rickey, Terrance, and Jacolvy would break the plating sequence into three steps. Jacolvy would start the plate with a circle of potato-parsnip puree and a half-ladle of sauce. Terrance would lay down the meat. Rickey would finish the plate with more sauce, a scatter of kirsch-plumped cherries, and the side veg—in this case, a small heap of garlic-sautéed kale—and top it with a metal hat that would keep the food hot and allow the waiters to stack plates three high on their big trays. On the other side, Tanker, Marquis, and Devonte would be doing the exact same thing. If the plates went out in ten rounds of thirty, Rickey figured they could serve each course in about seven minutes. You didn't want to have some people still waiting for a course while the guest of honor's table was taking the last bite.

"We're good to go," Rickey announced. He pulled two six-packs of beer out of one of the fridges and handed the frosty bottles around. He didn't actually want cooks working drunk, but because he'd come up with the idea for Liquor after he and

G-man had been fired for drinking beer in the kitchen at a crappy French Quarter tourist joint, he made a point of doing this at important moments. It was part good-luck charm, part positive reinforcement: a way of saying *I trust you enough to buy you a beer* before *your shift, not just after.*

"I was just gonna do some burgers or something for staff meal," G-man said as they finished their beers, "but how about we go across the street instead? That diner over there looked good."

"What, the Palace Café?" Rickey nodded. "That place is famous. Calvin Trillin wrote about it, I think. Well, sure, long as we can get back here by five-thirty or so, we should be fine."

They walked into the banquet hall, where waiters had begun setting and decorating long tables, and through the lobby to the street. A young policeman stood outside the theater looking half scared, half mad. As the seven cooks emerged, he held up a hand. "No foot traffic on the street right now. We got us a situation here."

"A what?" Rickey said.

"A God-Damn clusterfuck!" Schexnaydre yelled. Rickey hadn't seen him come up, but here he was, baring his teeth and glowering at the young cop. The policeman tried to wave him back, but Schexnaydre barreled right past him. "Piss the hell off, you little pissant! We got a Ducks Unlimited banquet starting in three hours and no time for this bullshit!"

"Sir, this is a potential terrorist situation—"

"The fuck it is! This is another one of Harry Comeaux's goddamn war games. All I got to say is he better wrap it up *real* soon or he's gonna have the sportsmen of St. Landry Parish to answer to. Now get out of my way—I'm taking these gentlemen over to the Palace!"

"Sir—"

Schexnaydre actually growled at the cop, a low wordless sound, and the poor guy took a step backward. Like a row of baby ducklings, the cooks followed Schexnaydre across the street. Just as they got to the other side, an armored personnel carrier draped in American flags rounded the corner of the courthouse square and trundled right past them. A small gray-haired man with thick glasses sat atop it, holding a rifle and staring straight ahead. "Comeaux, you stupid piece of shit!" Schexnaydre hollered, shaking his fist, but the little man's steely gaze never wavered.

They entered the Palace Café—a dim, high-ceilinged place that looked as if it hadn't changed much since 1953 or so—and took two tables. Rickey ended up with G-man, Tanker, Marquis, and Schexnaydre. "What the hell's going on?"

"Our Chief of Police." Schexnaydre spat out the words as if they were drops of bile. "Another one of his damn Homeland Security drills. You probably read about 'em in the New Orleans papers—they love to print stuff that makes us look like a bunch of dumb coonasses. Comeaux gives 'em plenty of material. He wants to make sure we're up to snuff just in case Osama bin Laden ever decides to hit Opelousas."

"Y'all got a big Israeli population or something?" Tanker said.

"They got the Jew department store over in Eunice, but I don't know of any others. All the damn fool really wants to do is show off that tank of his. Last time he did this, he ran it into a brand-new police cruiser. Totaled it."

The cooks sneaked glances at each other as they scanned the menu. Finally Rickey said, "What about the banquet?"

"Well, all of us still gonna be there, of course, but right now Harry Asshole Comeaux's got the town airspace under no-fly orders. Lord only knows what time Bobby Hebert'll be able to get in, if he can make it at all."

Rickey's stomach rolled over. "I told you so," he whispered to G-man. "I knew something awful was going to happen."

"It hasn't happened yet," G-man murmured back. "Try to relax. Get you something to eat."

Rickey scanned the menu. It looked great, lots of old-fashioned Cajun, Creole, and diner-style dishes of the kind you either didn't see in New Orleans anymore or you saw costing $27 and tasting like crap. Here, the most expensive item on the menu was the "heavy beef T-bone" at $13.95. Just as he'd almost decided on the shrimp etouffée, he saw a red-faced man in a white bathrobe and an Arab headdress entering the restaurant. The guy looked about as embarrassed as anybody Rickey had ever laid eyes on. "Say, Miz Tina, you think I could get a glass of iced tea?" he asked the lady at the cash register.

The lady sighed. "Chief's doing one of his drills again, huh?"

"Yeah, and I'm supposed to say some kinda hummina-hummina and set off this damn—scuse me—this darn suicide bomb, but I'm awful thirsty."

Miz Tina signaled to one of the waitresses, who brought the guy a glass of tea. He drained it quickly and walked back across the street looking resigned.

"How's the etouffée?" Rickey asked the waitress.

"It's—" She tried not to turn her head as a loud bang and a series of pops came from the direction of the square. "It's real good. You get two vegetables with it, but we're out of the candied yams."

Somebody in the square was shouting through a bullhorn. Rickey couldn't make out the words. The waitress pressed her lips together so tight that all the color left them for a moment, then lifted her chin resolutely and smiled at the cooks. "And don't forget to save room for our baklava," she said. "We make it with fresh pecans."

* * *

The meal was superlative: the etouffée subtly spiced, the vegetables perfectly seasoned, the baklava rich with butter and brown sugar. Rickey grew further demoralized, as he always did when faced with a restaurant meal in which he couldn't pinpoint a single flaw. He didn't want *bad* meals—well, not unless dining at the restaurant of a chef he secretly hated—but picking at tiny flaws in other people's cooking made him more secure in his own abilities. It wasn't a trait he was particularly proud of, but so far he'd been unable to conquer it.

G-man, who harbored what Rickey considered an unreasonable disdain for phyllo, bucked the baklava trend by ordering the chocolate cream pie. He was still scraping his fork over the plate when Rickey glanced at the clock on his cell phone and said, "OK, we gotta get back."

"Let's hope the damn streets are safe for human habitation," said Schexnaydre, who'd just had a cup of shrimp and okra gumbo. He'd be having gumbo again later, at the banquet, but that didn't seem to bother him any.

There was no further sign of the armored personnel carrier or the man in the Arab headdress. The courthouse square was eerily deserted, but maybe it always got like that after the downtown workers had gone home; most of Opelousas' nightlife seemed to take place on the outskirts. The pork smell had begun to settle over the town again. Back in the kitchen, Rickey reviewed everybody's mise-en-place, checked the plates, made sure the gumbo was hot but not scorching. He set up two big rondeaus of his butter-poaching liquid and, along with Tanker, began par-cooking the drum. Butter-poaching was a technique recently made trendy by California chef Thomas Keller. Unlike most trendy techniques, Rickey thought it had a lot of merit. Keller posited that cooking seafood too fast—"violently" was the word he used—caused it to seize up and fail to retain flavor. By poaching the seafood very slowly in an emulsion of butter, white wine, stock, and shallots, it was possible to retain a texture nearly as lush and silken as that of raw seafood. Rickey and Tanker cooked three hundred pieces of fish to just a hair below done, wrapped them in the duck prosciutto, and stored them in hotel pans. They'd crisp them off in the ovens later, just before it was time to serve the course.

The task took a fair amount of concentration. Rickey was glad, as it took his mind off the approaching evening. His heart was no longer in the event, but he knew he had to overcome that attitude. Even if Bobby Hebert never showed up, there were 299 other guests who deserved a great meal.

He wanted another beer, but decided against it. He'd already had a second one over at the Palace, and he didn't need a third. His mind had to be absolutely clear for this event. Thirty minutes until the diners were seated. He held up a hand in front of his face to see if it was shaking. Nope, rock-steady. But where the hell was G-man? That was all he needed now, his key cook disappearing. Maybe he'd just gone to the bathroom or something. Here he came now, walking back into the kitchen with Tee Fontenot and…who was that tall guy behind them? Rickey blinked, shook his head, looked again.

"Chef!" said Fontenot. "Where you at? Got somebody wants to meet you!"

G-man folded his arms across his chest and leaned against the counter looking pleased with himself, as if maybe he'd helped Fontenot fly the helicopter that had finally brought the guest of honor here.

"It's a pleasure to meet you," said Bobby Hebert, grasping Rickey's hand in both of his own. "Man, I don't know how you chefs do it, coming up with all these great recipes. Must be hard work, huh?"

Rickey looked up into those dark, slightly hollow eyes, shook the hand that had thrown the ball that had first made him think about his purpose in life, felt his knees weaken, tried to tamp down the huge, goofy grin that wanted to spread across his face. "Yeah, I guess it's pretty hard," he said. "No big deal. I been doing it all my life."

XVI

LE FER DANS LE LIT

I t was going to be a long time before G-man let him forget that nonchalant *I guess it's pretty hard.* For weeks, months, possibly years, Rickey knew he'd be listening to variations of the line: *Ovooo, yeah, Bobby, it's pretty hard awright, especially when I look at youuuuuuuu.* Rickey didn't care. He visited the head table three times during the course of the evening, listening to the Cajun Cannon rave about his menu.

"Man, I gotta tell you I never thought a New Orleans cook could make a great duck and sausage gumbo – that's a Cajun thing. You got it right, though. Tastes like you grew up on the bayou."

The other people at the table nodded, and Rickey breathed a small inward sigh of relief. He was confident about his other courses, but he hadn't been sure he was capable of making a gumbo that would wow this crowd.

A little later: "That's the best duck I ever had, that teal! It's a lean bird, how you got it so tender?"

Rickey leaned over, put his hand on Bobby's shoulder—trying not to notice the hard pad of muscle there, but he could n't quite help it—and spoke his secret directly into Bobby's ear.

"Wrapped it in bacon, then threw the bacon away. You like the cherries with it?"

"Yeah, yeah, yeah! I think I taste a little liquor in there—that's what y'all do, huh? I'm gonna have to check out your restaurant."

"You do that. We'll take real good care of you."

"So how you like the Saints this year, Chef?"

"I like 'em a lot." The team had been on a rare winning streak and was currently 11-4 with a good chance at a playoff berth.

G-man came out with him to help deliver the palate cleansers. Rickey didn't believe in chefs serving diners, had never done it even once in his career, but tonight he made an exception. They placed the soup spoons containing green sorbet balls in front of Bobby, Tee Fontenot, Schexnaydre, and another man they didn't know, and were just turning to go back to the kitchen when the entire crowd stood up and gave them a thunderous round of applause. Cries of "Speech! Speech!" and the sound of stomping feet rang through the hall.

G-man patted Rickey on the back. "Go on, you heard 'em. Share your genius, genius."

Rickey hunched his shoulders and made his way to the front of the hall, where a zydeco band was playing. The guitars and accordions trailed off and the singer relinquished the microphone.

"Uh, thanks," Rickey said. "I think this might be the only place I ever been where people like eating more than they do in New Orleans."

That was good for another prolonged round of applause. "*C'est si bon!*" somebody shouted.

"I wasn't gonna talk about this, but I got a little story I'd like to tell you. Just a real short one before you get your dessert. The month I turned thirteen, I went to my first Saints game in the Louisiana Superdome…"

The story went over well. Even with the bright stage lights in his face, Rickey could see Bobby Hebert's wide white smile when he finished it. Suddenly embarrassed, he hurried back to the kitchen door, where G-man was waiting for him.

"Why aren't you in there helping them set up the crème brûlées?"

"I wanted to hear what you had to say. You're a natural."

"Yeah, a natural dork. I was shit-scared."

"Dude, you sounded great and they loved it. I bet Bobby comes in to eat within the month."

Rickey braced his hands on the counter and let his shoulders droop. He realized he was exhausted. "You know what?" he said. "Except for the band, we're the only black people here."

"I hate to tell you this," said Terrance, "but y'all ain't black."

G-man waved a dismissive hand. "You know what your problem is, T? You're always getting caught up in the minor details."

"It's kinda weird, though, huh?" Rickey said. "Opelousas seems like a pretty black town, but we got an all-white crowd in here."

"Are Cajuns white?" Terrance asked. "I thought they got themselves declared a separate race or something."

"Look like a buncha crackers to me," Marquis volunteered.

"Just your basic crackers with boudin," Rickey said. It was a lame joke, but it struck him as funny, and suddenly he was howling with laughter.

"Oh my God, he's hysterical again," said G-man. "Go calm down somewhere, huh? Fantasize about Bobby Hebert. We got the desserts covered."

"Fuck that." Rickey caught his breath and resumed his place on the line. "I started this dinner, I'll finish it. Tanker, where's the damn duck skin triangles?"

After the desserts had gone out, Rickey tucked into a crème brûlée he'd saved for himself. He didn't have much of a sweet tooth, but he wanted to see how these had turned out. The sweet cream was unctuous with the flavor of duck fat, smooth and golden-tasting on the tongue. In lesser hands than Tanker's it could easily have been a disgusting mess, but the ramekins were already beginning to come back into the kitchen scraped clean. Rickey closed his eyes. They had done it. In the great Liquor tradition, they hadn't known a damn thing about what they were getting into, and they had done it anyway.

★ ★ ★

The banquet was just enough of a success. The party afterward was way too much of one.

Rickey had always thought he could drink. No, screw that; he *knew* he could drink. These people, though, put him to shame. He never finished his first glass of Wild Turkey, because it was always refilled before he got more than halfway through. Bobby Hebert had already left, which was probably just as well. The last thing Rickey remembered was Tee Fontenot telling him a long, convoluted joke about a mother listening at the bedroom door on her daughter's wedding night. It seemed the daughter had chronic cold feet and liked to sleep with a hot iron in the bed. The joke was mostly in English, but its humor seemed to hinge upon the fact that the phrases "the iron" (*le fer*) and "do it" (*le faire*) sounded alike in French. The punchline was, "Well, if he doesn't want to do it in the bed, then do it on the floor!" Rickey knew he'd laughed himself nearly sick over this incomprehensibility, and he was pretty sure he'd countered with a joke about Superman drinking in a bar, but the rest of the evening was a bourbon-soaked blur.

He woke up the next morning in the motel bathroom, curled half on a very thin towel, half on the cold floor with the tiles imprinting themselves into his skin. For several minutes he was utterly unable to get up even though he knew water and aspirin would be attainable if he did. When he finally managed it, he caught sight of himself in the mirror and gave a little cry of anguish. Snarled hair, red eyes, stubble, thousand-yard stare. How far he had fallen since last night!

G-man was sprawled on the bed, fully clothed and snoring. Rickey lowered his head carefully onto a pillow. The motion woke G-man. "Oh, God," he whispered. "What did they *do* to us?"

"Just acted like themselves, I guess." Rickey's tongue was sticking to the roof of his mouth. He wished he had some more water, but couldn't bring himself to get back up.

"Never again."

"Drinking?"

"Drinking with Cajuns."

"Good idea." Rickey tried to roll over, but an astounding bolt of pain shot through his head and he abandoned the effort. "I bet they're not even hung over."

"Damn," said G-man.

"What?"

"This was supposed to be our touristy day. We were gonna eat boudin."

Rickey groaned.

"Maybe by tonight we'll be ready for a link or two."

Rickey fought his gorge, failed, leaned over the edge of the bed, and threw up on the carpet. He knew this was a disgraceful thing to do, but it was mostly drool, and the carpet clearly had previous acquaintance with such things.

By late afternoon, they felt almost human. It was Sunday and the Palace Café was closed, as was almost everything else in town. They finally found a meat market and sat outside in their car, drinking cold Cokes and squeezing boudin into their mouths. The pork, rice, and green onion filling whose very mention had made them ill this morning now tasted indescribably wonderful. They ate two links apiece and threw the rubbery casings out the window for a dog who was hanging around the parking lot. Rickey looked down at the shiny white paper spread across his lap, marked with cayenne-red grease spots and the scrawled price of the sausage. "I think I could eat another one," he said.

"Better not push your luck."

"How about we buy a cooler and take some home?"

"Sure, and some andouille too."

Rickey's heart lifted as they walked back into the market and scanned the porcine bounty in the display case: sausages, thick-cut bacon, Styrofoam bowls of hogshead cheese, the stuffed pigs' stomachs known variously as *chaudin* or *ponce.* He remembered shaking Bobby Hebert's hand (maybe hanging on a bit too long, but he didn't think the Cannon had noticed), remembered Bobby saying *I'm gonna have to check out your restaurant.* If you didn't consider a day-long hangover a real set-back—which neither of them did—then the trip had been a great triumph.

XVII

JINGLE, JANGLE, JINGLE

On the night before the night before Christmas, Rickey and G-man decided to spend their evening off at Celebration in the Oaks, the big light show in City Park. Millions of colored lights were arranged in the shape of holiday scenes as well as things that seemed to have nothing to do with Christmas: circuses, dinosaurs, jazz bands. It was mostly a drive-through deal, but the best section was in the middle of the park, where you could leave your car and walk through the Botanical Garden and Storyland. Storyland was a fixture of every New Orleanian's childhood. It had a Tilt-A-Whirl and bumper cars and a merry-go-round the old folks called "flying horses," but what made it unique was the garden of brightly painted statues from fairy tales and nursery rhymes. The wolf from Little Red Riding Hood lurked in a playhouse, granny-capped and fear-somely befanged. A topless, slightly pornographic Little Mermaid sat on a rock in the middle of a small pond. Mother Goose swooped down from a low-hanging oak branch, looking as if she might snatch up a kid or two. There were things kids could climb and slide down and fall off of, and it was all just the tiniest bit macabre, as any great children's amusement should be.

The Saints had won their final game of the season the previous Sunday, beating the hated Atlanta Falcons, finishing with a 12-4 record, and securing a spot in the playoffs, something that was a big deal for any football team but a rare and shining moment for New Orleans. Rickey was ready to celebrate. The evening was cold, not painfully so but enough to feel like Christmas. He bought two cups of hot buttered rum that turned out to be nonalcoholic and foul, but he didn't care. Everything seemed magical.

Near the kiddie rollercoaster, they came upon another relic of their childhoods: a two-story sculpture of Mr. Bingle suspended from the branches of a live oak. Mr. Bingle had started life as a Christmas advertisement for the Maison Blanche department store downtown, but soon became a beloved New Orleans star. He was sort of an assistant to Santa, a little snowman with a red nose, an ice-cream-cone hat, and wings of holly. A flying snowman with holly wings didn't really make sense, but New Orleans kids had no idea what a snowman was supposed to look like. At the height of his popularity, he'd spawned dolls, a TV show, and a sparkly winter wonderland in the department store's display window.

This particular Mr. Bingle had made annual appearances flying high above Canal Street on the store façade, but fell into disrepair and obscurity when Maison Blanche sold out to a national chain. He'd spent the last several years in a warehouse somewhere in the Lower Ninth Ward. This year a group of Bingle lovers had taken up a collection to restore him and make him part of Celebration in the Oaks. The sound of the theme song pouring out of hidden speakers made Rickey's throat tighten. His memories of Mr. Bingle weren't entirely good—he remembered being five years old, sitting in the living room watching a Maison Blanche TV commercial while his parents fought in their bedroom—but, like every other New

Orleans kid born between the fifties and the seventies, he felt a helpless, sentimental wave of nostalgia for the little snowman.

Jingle, jangle, jingle,
Here comes Mr. Bingle
With another message from Kris Kringle
Time to launch your Christmas season
Maison Blanche makes Christmas pleasin'
Gifts galore for you to see
Each a gem from…MB!

As he stood blinking at the utter familiarity of the slightly mechanical ladies' voices—voices he hadn't heard in nearly thirty years—Rickey felt someone tap him on the shoulder. He turned and saw Shake Vojtaskovic arm in arm with a gorgeous, dreadlocked black girl.

"Hey, Snake," he said.

"Hey, Pudge."

"That what they're calling me now?"

"So I hear."

Rickey found that he didn't care. Shake had most likely made up the nickname, and even if he hadn't, nobody trusted a skinny chef. "Who's your friend?" he said.

"Oh…this is Lila. She tends bar at La Pharmacie. Lila, this is Rickey."

"Not Pudge?" the girl said in what sounded like a Jamaican accent.

Rickey shrugged. "Rickey, Pudge, dickhead, whatever you like."

Lila laughed, but not unkindly.

"You're in a good mood," Shake observed.

"Yeah. Things are going good." Rickey started to launch into a litany of boasts, then decided not to bother. What was the point? He knew what he'd done, and he no longer had anything to prove to Shake. "I hear good stuff about your place, too."

"Yeah. Some of it's probably even true. Things weren't all that great at first, but they're getting better." Shake glanced at Lila, who smiled back at him. "Plus I just got a great new sous chef who really knows what he's doing. Y'all ought to come in sometime. We'll do it up for you."

"I will," Rickey promised. Maybe he even would. He didn't expect much of La Pharmacie, but it would be nice to see an alumnus of his kitchen putting out good food. There was no point in making more enemies than you had to.

And whatever else he might do, he now felt certain that he could cook duck in more different and delicious ways than any other chef in the city. He was already planning a tasting menu that reprised the Ducks Unlimited banquet, with variations to accommodate domestic ducks and the boozy requirements of Liquor.

He and G-man talked to Shake and his new lady for a few minutes more, then continued on their way. As they walked into the Botanical Garden, an endless array of tiny lights seemed to stretch before them, multicolored and dazzling, repeated in the long reflecting pool. Stars were never visible in the night sky here, only the purple glow that hung over any brightly lit city, but this must be how they would look if you could see them. Things to count, even though counting them all was impossible. Things to wish on.

In the panoramic shimmer of lights, water, and sky, Rickey thought he could glimpse the future: true love, great food, Bobby Hebert coming to eat at his restaurant, the Saints winning the Super Bowl, the city of New Orleans standing whole, strong, beautiful forever.